'There's something I had to tell you,' Ava said.

'Si?' Gianluca asked.

'This isn't the first time we've met.'

'Is that so?'

'I don't seem...familiar to you?'

He shrugged.

Ava knew right then that any chance of her making a little joke of it, or him being enchanted, or curious, or even maybe a little regretful had evaporated.

'I meet many people. Forgive me if I don't recall your face.'

His tone was reasonable, his words polite. But the sentiments—they stung...

I don't recall your face. I don't remember lying in the grass on Palatine Hill cradling you in my arms. I don't remember a single one of the personal confessions you made because, really, it meant nothing to me.

'You really don't remember?' she persevered.

A look of irritation flashed across those hooded eyes.

'No doubt you will tell me.'

Ava knew it was irrational. She knew she had no right to expect something so fleeting, so long ago, to have stayed with him as it had with her. She hadn't realised until that moment how deep she was into this fantasy. She really had to stop it now—unless she was keen on full shake-down humiliation.

'I'm waiting,' he said.

Lucy Ellis has four loves in life: books, expensive lingerie, vintage films and big, gorgeous men who have to duck going through doorways. Weaving aspects of them into her fiction is the best part of being a romance writer. Lucy lives in a small cottage in the foothills outside Melbourne.

Recent titles by the same author:

A DANGEROUS SOLACE

BY
LUCY ELLIS

First published in Great Britain 2013
by Mills & Boon, an imprint of Harlequin (UK) Limited.
Harlequin (UK) Limited, Eton House, 18-24 Paradise Road,
Richmond, Surrey TW9 1SR

© Lucy Ellis 2013

ISBN: 978 0 263 23572 2

Printed and bound in Great Britain
by CPI Antony Rowe, Chippenham, Wiltshire

A DANGEROUS SOLACE

CHAPTER ONE

GIANLUCA BENEDETTI APPRAISED the shapeless suit and then the woman in it. She had potential, if she ditched the floppy large-brimmed hat, took down her hair, stepped out of the suit and started all over again from scratch. She had the essentials. She was tall, her legs were good from what he could tell, and there was a liveliness to her that she seemed to be repressing as she went to stamp her foot but then arrested the gesture.

Which drew his attention to her shoes. They didn't quite fit the image of the woman wearing them. Elegant low heels, graceful arch, red leather slingback, with a complicated knot of red silk flowers running over the toes. The shoes were fussy and feminine. The woman in them was not.

'Give me back my money!' Her voice was clear, crisp and no-nonsense, for all she was obviously angry. Gianluca could tell by her accent she was Australian, which accounted for the plain speaking.

The guy was giving her the runaround. In the crowded do-main of the arcade people were making a detour around the brunette standing in front of the kiosk. She looked like a tick-ing time bomb ready to go off.

The foot trembling with indecision above the pavement came down with a decided stamp.

'I am not going anywhere until you refund me that money. I gave your company forty-eight hours' notice. It says clearly on your website that refunds are possible with *twenty-four hours'* notice.'

Gianluca shut down the European markets, pocketed his personal device, and strolled away from the doorway of the coffee bar he'd been frequenting all his adult life in Rome.

Impeccable manners towards women instilled in him by a Sicilian grandmother had him approach her.

'*Signora*, may I be of some service to you?'

She didn't even bother to turn around. 'I am not a *signora*, I am a *signorina*. And no, you may not *help me*. I'm perfectly capable of helping myself. Go and ply your trade with some other idiot tourist.'

Gianluca leaned closer. She emitted a light fragrance, something floral, definitely too feminine for this dragon of a woman.

'My trade?'

'Gigolo. Escort. Servicer of women. Go away. I don't want you.'

Gianluca stilled. This dragon thought he was a male prostitute?

He looked her up and down. She hadn't even bothered to turn around. Common sense told him to shrug and walk away.

'So, *signorina*…' he laid on the emphasis '…maybe you're hard up, yes? You need to remember what it is to be a woman?'

'Excuse me?' She turned around, angling up her face, and in a single stroke Gianluca lost every preconception he had built around her.

The shapeless clothes, her tone—he'd taken her to be older, harder…certainly less attractive than—*this*. She had creamy skin, wide brows, amazing cheekbones and—what was most intriguing—soft, lush lips. A veritable ripe strawberry of a mouth. But her face was dominated by a pair of ugly white-rimmed sunglasses, and he had to resist the urge to tug them away and get the full effect.

Although he definitely got a sense of her eyes widening.

'It's you!' she said.

He raised a brow. 'Have we met?'

This wasn't an unknown scenario over the years. His past football career—two years of kicking a ball around professionally for Italy—combined with his title had given him something of a public profile beyond the usual roaming grounds of Roman society. He made sure his tone offered no encouragement.

The dragon-who-wasn't took a step back.

'No,' she said fast, as if warding him off.

He became aware that she was looking around as if searching for an escape route, and for some reason his own body tensed. He recognised he was readying himself to give chase.

Madre di Dio, what was going on?

A pulse pounded like a tiny drum at the base of her throat, and he couldn't have said why but it held his attention. She made a soft sound of panic. His eyes flicked up to catch hers and sexual awareness erupted between them. It was so fast, so strong, it took him entirely off guard.

He stepped towards her, but she didn't shift an inch. Her chin tipped up and her eyes flared wide, as if she was waiting for something.

Something from *him*.

Something he couldn't quite put his finger on.

Basta! This was getting him nowhere.

Irritated by his own unprecedented behaviour—getting involved with a strange woman on the street, allowing his libido to get away from him, lingering as if he had the day to while away when he had a meeting lined up across town—he did what he should have done when he'd emerged from the coffee bar five minutes ago.

'In that case, enjoy your stay in Rome, *signorina*.'

He'd only gone a few steps when he found himself turning around.

She was still standing there, swamped by that god-awful jacket and wearing those trousers which did nothing for her, and yet...

He was noticing other things about her—the pink of her

nose, the slightly hectic expression on her face. She'd been crying.

It stirred something in him. A memory.

A weeping woman usually left him cold. He knew all about female manipulation. He'd grown up observing it with his mother and sisters. Tears were usually a woman's go-to device for getting her own way. It never ceased to amaze him how a pretty bauble or a promise could dry them up.

But instead of walking away he strode over to the kiosk, read the sign that told him this was Fenice Tours, which was run by a subsidiary of the travel conglomerate Benedetti International had business with, and took out his phone. As he thumbed in the number he told the guy he had sixty seconds to refund the *turista* for her ticket or he'd close the place down.

With a few more well-placed instructions he handed over his phone. The man took it with a sceptical look that faded as his employer's angry voice buzzed like a blowfly on the other end.

'*Mi scusi, Principe.* It was a—a misunderstanding,' the guy stammered.

Gianluca shrugged. 'Apologise to the lady, not to me.'

'*Si, si—scusa tanto, signora.*'

With gritted teeth she accepted the euros. For all the fuss she had made, Gianluca noticed she didn't bother to check them, just folded them silently into her bag—a large leather affair that, like her clothes, seemed to be part of an attempt to weigh herself down.

'*Grazie,*' she said, as if it were torn from her.

There was no reason to linger. Gianluca was at the kerb opening up his low-slung Lamborghini Jota when he looked back.

She had followed him and was watching him, her expression almost comical in its war between curiosity and resentment—and something else...

It was the *something else* that kept him from jumping into the car.

She seemed to gird herself before walking over.

'Excuse me.' Her voice was as stiff as her manner, but it didn't take away from the rather lovely combination of her full mouth and dramatic cheekbones, or the way her caution made her seem oddly prim. It was the stiff formality that had his eyes locked to hers.

'I'm curious,' she said.

He could feel her gaze searching his face as if hunting for something. Curious, but not thankful, he noted, amused despite the wariness that told him something about this wasn't right.

'Could you really have shut it down?'

She angled up a stubborn chin made somewhat less forth-right by the soft press of a dimple and hard suspicion narrowed his gaze.

Where had he seen that gesture before?

Yet he gave her a tight smile, a smile that didn't reach his eyes—the one he handed out to women as a courtesy, telling them he recognised that they were female, and as a man he appreciated it, but alas it could go no further.

'*Signorina,*' he drawled, 'this is Rome. I'm a Benedetti. Anything's possible.'

He was pushing through the mess that was Rome's mid-morning traffic when her reaction registered. She hadn't looked flattered. She hadn't even looked shocked. She had looked furiously angry.

And against his better judgement it had him turning the car around.

CHAPTER TWO

AVA STOOD AT the kerb as the low-slung sports machine vanished into the traffic and let shock reverberate through her body until the only thing left was the burn.

Benedetti.

All she could think was that this wasn't how it was supposed to happen.

Over the years she'd had a few false alarms—moments when a deep voice, an Italian accent, a pair of broad shoulders had brought her head snapping around, her senses suddenly firing. But reality would always intervene.

Clearly reality had decided to slap her in the face.

It came over her in a rush. The flick of a broad tanned wrist at the ignition of a growling Ducati motorcycle. The tightening of her arms around his muscle-packed waist as they made their getaway from a wedding he'd had no interest in and she'd been cut up about. The memory of a flight into a summer's night seven long years ago that she still couldn't shake.

It was all Ava could do as she stood in the street to keep the images—those highly sexual images—at bay.

Finding herself in the early hours of a summer morning lying in the grass on the Palatine Hill, her dress rucked up around her waist, under the lean, muscular weight of a young Roman god come to life was *not* something a woman forgot in a hurry.

Finding herself repeating it an hour later, in a bed that had once belonged to a king, in a *palazzo* built literally for a princess, on a beautiful *piazza* in the centre of the city, and again and again into the first flush of dawn, was also something that had stayed with her. And all the while he had lavished her with praise in broken English, making her feel like a goddess he had every right to plunder.

In the glare of a new morning she had slipped from the palace unnoticed and, Cinderella-fashion, left her shoes behind in her haste to flee what had promised to be an awkward aftermath.

Her feet bare, her frothy blue dress hiked up around her knees to allow her to run, she had been in equal measure elated and a little *triste*, her body pleasurably aching from all the unfamiliar clenching of muscles she hadn't known she had.

She'd flagged down a taxi and driven away, and if she had looked back it had been only to fix the memory, because she'd known it would never happen again.

It had been a moment out of time.

She'd flown back to Sydney the next day, resumed her climb up the corporate ladder and assumed she would never see him again.

Clearly she had assumed wrongly.

Pulling herself together, Ava stepped away from the kerb and told herself she most definitely wasn't going to allow the memory of one night with a Ducati-straddling, over-sexed soccer player to wreak havoc with her plans. She'd been handling everything so well up until this point.

Perhaps too well, niggled her conscience as she battled her way along the pavement. Wasn't she supposed to be heartbroken?

Most women would be. Being dumped on the eve of expecting a proposal from your long-time boyfriend in a foreign city and then travelling on in that city on your own would unsettle anybody.

Fortunately she was made of sterner stuff.

Which was why she was on her way to the Spanish Steps, to join a tour of literary sites in Rome.

Ava pulled her hat down hard on top of her head. She certainly wasn't going to allow a freak sighting of one of Italy's natural wonders in a city street to derail her from her purpose.

So what if that puffy pale blue bridesmaid's dress was buried deep in the back of her closet at home? So she'd kept the dress? So she was in Rome?

It had nothing to do with that long-ago night when everything she'd believed about herself had been turned on its head.

Well, not this time. Nowadays she had it all under control—when she wasn't careering hot-headedly around the streets of Rome looking for the...what was it...? She consulted her map. The Piazza di Spagna.

She ignored the racing of her heart, told herself there was *no way* she was going to fumble through an Italian phone directory searching for the address of the Palazzo Benedetti. She mustn't even *think* that! Rome had definitely been a mistake. The sooner she picked up that hire car tomorrow and headed north the better.

Now—Ava looked around in confusion, discovering she had walked into a square she didn't recognise—where on earth was she?

'This is *pazzo*,' Gianluca muttered under his breath as he idled his car across from the little *piazza*. He'd followed her. He'd put the Jota into a screaming U-turn and cruised after that flapping hat, those flashing red shoes.

Inferno, what was he doing? He was Gianluca Benedetti. He didn't kerb-crawl a woman. And not *this* kind of female—one who wore men's trousers and a silk shirt buttoned up to her chin and seemed to have no conception of what it was to be a woman.

Many women had creamy skin, long legs, and if they did not have quite the drama of her bone structure they certainly did a lot more with it.

She wasn't his type. Yet here he was.

He could see her pacing backwards and forwards over the cobblestones, holding something aloft. He got the impression it was a map from the way she was positioning it.

His phone vibrated. He palmed it.

'Where are you?' Gemma's voice was faintly exasperated. *Stalking a turista.*

'Stuck in traffic.'

He glanced at the piece of Swiss design on his arm. He was extremely late. *What in the hell was he doing?*

'What do I tell the clients?'

'Let them cool their heels. I'm on my way.'

He pocketed the phone and made up his mind. As he strode across the *piazza* he wondered at the complication he was inviting into his life.

She was walking slowly backwards, clearly trying to get the name of the square from a plaque on the wall above her. He could have saved her the effort and told her she'd have no luck there. It was the name of the building.

She careened into him.

'Oh, I do beg your pardon,' she trotted out politely, reeling around.

The good manners, he noted, were for other people.

It was his last half-amused thought as he collided with her eyes. One part of his brain wondered if they were coloured contact lenses—except judging by the rest of her attire he doubted she'd go to the trouble.

No, the eye colour was hers, all right. An extraordinary sea-green. One of those colours that changed with the light or her mood. Eyes that shoved the rock out of the mouth of the cave inside him he'd had sealed up for many years. Eyes and a mouth, and a soft, yielding body which she had taken away from him when he had needed it most.

Her features coalesced around those unusual eyes and the impact fairly slammed into him. The other part of his brain was free-falling.

'*You!*'

His sentiments exactly.

The softer note in her voice long gone, she leapt back in horror. But he noticed at the same time that she wrapped her hand around his arm, as if anchoring herself to him. Which struck him as entirely ironic, given the last time he'd laid eyes on this girl she'd been so anxious to escape from his bed she'd left her shoes behind in her rush.

From nowhere a resentment he hadn't known he was carrying ricocheted like a stray bullet around his body.

What in the hell was she doing back in Rome? Back in his life?

His eyes narrowed on her.

'Are you following me?' she accused swiftly.

'*Si.*' He was not going to deny it. Why would he?

The look on her face was priceless.

'You appear to be lost, *signorina*,' he observed smoothly, raking his gaze over her eyes, her mouth, the amazing clarity of her skin. 'And as we already know one another—'

If anything the rapt horror on her face only increased, heightening his sense of satisfaction.

'Allow me to offer some more assistance.'

She tugged self-consciously at the atrocious silk shirt and stood a little straighter, sticking out that chin.

He was going to enjoy making her squirm, and then he would let her go.

'Is this a profession for you? Following women around the city, pushing help on them whether they want it or not?'

'You appear to be the exception to my rule to let a woman struggle on alone.'

'Do I appear to be struggling to you?'

'No, you appear to be lost.'

She pursed her lips, staring rather pointedly at the map. She was torn—it was all over her expressive face. The indecision and—more satisfying to his ego—anxiety.

Gianluca told himself a sensible man would walk away.

Anything between them now was beneath him. He'd made the identification. He knew exactly who this woman was—or who she purported to be. Seven years ago he'd entwined all kinds of ridiculous romantic imaginings around this girl, none of them bearing scrutiny in the harsh light of day.

Besides, on *this* day she was proving entirely ordinary—a little frumpy, in fact. Certainly not a woman he would glance at twice. Which didn't explain why he'd turned the Jota around and right now was unable to take his eyes off her.

'It's too late now anyhow,' she muttered to herself.

Si, far too late. Although unexpectedly he was fighting a very Italian male need to assert himself with this woman.

'I've missed the start of the tour,' she said, as if it was somehow his fault.

Gianluca waited.

She stared holes in the map.

'We're supposed to be meeting at the Spanish Steps,' she added grudgingly.

'I see.' Not that he did see.

He decided to cut to the chase and draw down the time this was taking.

'The Spanish Steps are straight down here.' He pointed it out. 'Make a left and then a second right.'

She was trying to follow his directions, which meant she was forced to look at him, and at the same time she was fumbling to put on her ugly sunglasses. Seeing as the sky was overcast, it was clearly a clumsy attempt at disguise.

Something about her hasty and long overdue attempt to hide irritated him. She clearly wasn't very good at subterfuge, and yet she had been a true genius at escape seven years ago. Gianluca found he was tempted to confiscate the glasses.

Safe behind the shaded lenses, she tipped up her glorious cheekbones. 'I suppose I should thank you.'

'Don't feel obligated, *signorina*,' he inserted softly.

Those lips pursed, but nothing could destroy their luscious shape.

Pushing aside the knowledge that this promised endless complications, he reached into his jacket and took out a card, took hold of her resistant hand and closed her fingers over it. They felt warm, smooth and surprisingly delicate.

She snatched her hand back and glared at him as if he'd touched her inappropriately.

A far cry from the last time he'd had his hands on her.

'If you change your mind about thanking me, *signorina*, I'll be at Rico's Bar tonight around eleven,' he said, wondering what the hell he thought he was doing. 'It's a private party but I'll leave your name at the door. Enjoy your tour.'

'You don't even know my name,' she called after him, and it sounded almost like an accusation.

His gut knotted.

Exactly. If he'd known her name seven years ago this little piece of unfinished business would have been forgotten.

Just another girl on another night.

But it hadn't been just another night.

It was a night scored on his soul, and the woman standing in the square was a major part of that. *Si*, it explained why his chest felt tight and his hands were clenched into fists by his sides.

Ruthlessness was in his blood, and Gianluca never forgot he was a Benedetti. In this fabled city it was impossible to forget. His ancestors had led Roman legions, lent money to Popes and financed wars down the ages. There was enough blood flowing through the family annals to turn the Tyrrhenian Sea red.

It enabled him to look at her with detachment.

'How about Strawberries?' he drawled. The quiet menace in his tone was usually enough to send CEOs of multinational corporations pale as milk.

She lowered the sunglasses and those green eyes skewered him.

A dark admiration stirred. This woman had the makings of a formidable opponent.

He could enjoy this.

Basta! This was no *vendetta*. She was, after all, a woman, and he—naturally—wasn't that kind of man. He was a chivalrous, civilised, honourable member of Roman society. This was merely an exercise in curiosity, in putting a footnote to a certain episode in his life. The first and only time a woman had run from him.

He slid into the Jota and gunned the engine.

The fact his knuckles showed white on the wheel proved nothing.

But as he merged with the chaotic traffic again he recognised it was not his Benedetti side that was in the ascendant here. It was the Sicilian blood from his mother's people, and it responded instinctively to the knowledge that this little piece of unfinished business was at last in his sights once more.

CHAPTER THREE

AVA FORCED HERSELF to block the encounter out of her head as she followed his directions and caught her first glimpse in seven years of the Spanish Steps. Despite the crowd she found her tour group and fastened on, all too aware she was already hot and tired and flustered.

He'd followed her.

Yes, but he likes women. That's his modus operandi. He sees a girl. He takes her.

He saw you, he wants you.

Ava tried to focus on what the guide was saying about Keats's death, but all she could think about was her own small death of pride, which had her desperately wanting to go to this club tonight, to see him again...

She shut her eyes and screwed up her resolve. She wasn't the kind of woman who slept with random men—and that was all it ever could be with a guy like Benedetti. A night, a hand-ful of hours—entertainment for him.

You liked it. He saw you. He wants you.

It wasn't any kind of reason for offering herself up to be hurt again.

It's not as if you've got anything to lose. You're a single woman and this is Rome.

For a moment her resolve slipped and her surroundings rushed in. For beyond the hurried crowd and the noise of traffic was the city itself, imprinted on her mind by countless Hollywood films. *Bella Italia*, where magical things were supposed to happen to single girls if they threw coins in fountains. And sometimes those things *did* happen—but this girl had misread the signs.

Every time she got it wrong. She wasn't going to get it wrong again.

Emotions welled up unexpectedly, filling her throat, making it difficult to breathe. She'd been crying again this morning and she *never* cried! Not even when Bernard had rung her three days ago, at the terminal in Sydney International an hour before take-off, to tell her he wouldn't be coming to Rome.

Just as her realisation had begun to take shape that there would be no romantic proposal in front of the Trevi Fountain, and before she could examine the overwhelming feeling of *relief* that had washed over her, he'd broken the news that he had found another woman—and that with *her* he had passion.

It had been a low blow, even for Bernard. He'd never been particularly sensitive to her feelings, but she had assumed up until that moment that half the blame for their lacklustre sex life was shared by him.

Apparently not. Apparently it was all down to her.

'Passion?' she had shouted down the phone. 'We could have had passion. In *Rome*!'

Yet ever since—on the long-haul flight, on the taxi ride from Fiumicino Airport to her historic hotel, over the two nights she'd spent staring at the walls as she listlessly ate her room-service dinner in front of the Italian melodrama she was just starting to get hooked on—Ava had nursed a suspicion that she had chosen Rome as the site of her proposal for entirely *romantic* reasons that clearly had nothing to do with Bernard.

She was beginning to suspect there were unplumbed depths of longing inside of her for a different life.

A romantic life.

But it was no use. Romance belonged in the movies, not in real life. Certainly not in *her* life. She'd learned that young, from watching the break-up of her parents' marriage, seeing her mentally ill mother struggle to support them on a pension, that the only way to survive as a woman was to become financially independent.

So she had worked hard to get where she was, but it meant she had never had time for a social life, had never gone through the rites of passage her peers had taken for granted.

As a consequence she had done a very silly thing seven years ago, and another silly thing when she'd convinced herself to marry a man she didn't love.

No, Bernard was not the right man for her. But neither was an oversexed soccer player who thought he could just pick up a woman like a coin in the gutter and put her in his pocket.

Her fist opened to reveal the embossed card she'd been carrying around for the last half hour. She held it up and read the simply inscribed name and several contact numbers. A memory slid like a stiletto knife between her ribs. All those numbers—but she'd rung his numbers before, hadn't she? None of them led to him.

Giving herself a shake, Ava slipped away from the group. She was going back to the hotel.

Everything was a mess and it was *his* fault.

Not Bernard's. What had she been thinking, being with Bernard for two long years? Going so far as to orchestrate a romantic proposal? Booking the plane fares, a luxury hotel, a driving tour of Tuscany…?

What had possessed her to set up such a ridiculous romantic scenario with a man she didn't love, in this city of all cities…?

Ava's heart began to pound, because she had the answer in her hot little hand.

What was she doing back in Rome?

It was the million-dollar question and it had Gianluca entertaining scenarios that, frankly, were beneath him.

Behind him the private party was in full swing—a welcome back to Rome for his cousin Marco and his new wife—

but Gianluca found himself constantly scanning the *piazza* below for a certain dressed-down brunette.

He hadn't been able to get her out of his head all day. It wasn't the fresh-faced girl who had lain down with him in the grass on the Palatino who was rifling through his thoughts, though, but the tense, angry woman who looked as if she hadn't had a man between her thighs in a good many years. The sort of woman who, for whatever reason, had forgotten how to *be* a woman—although in this lady's case he suspected it might be a wilful act.

He smiled slightly, wondered how hard it would be to perform that miracle.

Given the sexual attraction that had flared between them in the street today, not hard. Anger, he acknowledged, could be a powerful aphrodisiac.

His smile faded. His parents had conducted that kind of relationship. Volatile, glass-breaking performances on his Sicilian mother's side, and passive-aggressive acts of sabotage from his father as he withheld money, access to the family jewellery, use of the Benedetti *palazzi* dotted around the country. Yes, the married state had a great deal to recommend it.

The irony was that he was here celebrating a wedding. The advent of a baby. The things that made up happiness in other people's lives. Just not if you had Benedetti attached to your name.

It was a lonely thought and he pushed it aside. Life was good. He was young, fit and obscenely successful. Women fell at his feet. Men scrambled to get out of his way. Everything he touched turned to gold these days. Forget the dragon. Forget the past. Take those lessons and apply them to what was to come now.

He turned away from his contemplation of the famous square below and strolled across the terrace to join the party.

'*Signorina*, we sit here all night or I take you somewhere else? Give me something to work with!'

Across the road Ava could see women in tiny scraps of nothing much going happily into the popular nightspot. She shoved money at the driver, took a breath and launched herself out of the cab. The cool air licked around her legs and she almost dived back in.

She knew she was being silly. The burgundy red cocktail dress came to her knees and covered her shoulders and arms. It was perfectly acceptable. Perhaps it clung to her long thighs as she moved, and her calves in black stockings felt exposed as she made her way across the road, heels clicking on the pavement, but nobody was going to laugh at her and point.

As she approached the glass front of the upmarket nightclub she began to feel a little differently. The pulsing blue and gold neon lights gave a dreamlike quality to the atmosphere, and far from feeling on show she realised for once that with her hair and her dress and her heels she fitted right in. There was nothing show-offish about her appearance.

She had a very real fear of making a spectacle of herself in public. Growing up, she had seen her mum's illness provide far too many opportunities for that to happen. She had set up her life to avoid social situations as much as possible, but tonight she didn't have much choice.

The doorman said something pleasant to her in Italian and Ava found herself inside, waiting behind the other patrons, relieved she had dressed up. For the umpteenth time her fingers went to the ends of her hair.

This afternoon she'd taken her long brown plait to the hairdresser, and after a process of a great deal of pointing and gesturing her hair was now swinging with more bounce and life than it had ever had around her shoulders. She'd left that hairdresser feeling as chic as any Roman woman, very modern, and in control of her own destiny once more.

As with cutting several inches off her hair, it had been her choice to wear a cocktail dress. That it was brand-new, bought today, and she couldn't remember the last time she'd worn a frock had absolutely nothing to do with a man this morning telling her she had *forgotten how to be a woman.*

She couldn't see him anyhow as she came down the steps and made her way slowly through the crowded bar. Confusion assailed her. Should she wait? Should she ask for his table? Worryingly, the place seemed to be full of beautiful women not wearing very much clothing. She couldn't possibly compete.

As if to hammer this home a glamorous blonde slunk past her on stab-your-heart-out heels, scantily clad in a dress that looked sewn on. Ava followed her progress, along with every man in the vicinity, although her thoughts—*She must be cold*—probably didn't align with theirs.

Perhaps she'd over-estimated the transformative powers of a new hairstyle?

Feeling her confidence slipping away, Ava scanned the room, spotted the winding stairs at either end. There was another level. She caught sight of the blonde making her wiggly way up and up. Should she go upstairs? Should she ask for his table?

For the first time it occurred to Ava with a stab of unease that the invitation had been general, more along the lines of *come along—enjoy yourself.* Not specific—not *I find you attractive, perhaps even on some subliminal level remember you, and I want to spend some time with you.* It was entirely possible she had misinterpreted him.

Yes, Ava, you've got it wrong again...

But in that moment she caught sight of a dark-haired woman in a burgundy dress staring back at her across the room. Her eyes were made up with kohl and lashings of mascara, dark and mysterious, her mouth was a vivid splash of red colour like a full-blown rose, explosive and passionate. She was something other than beautiful. She was *dramatic.*

It wasn't until she lifted her fingertips once more to her hair that Ava experienced the little shock of recognition. It was a mirrored wall. The woman staring back at her was—well, *her.*

She ignored the thundering voices that told her she was lining herself up for a fall and made her way upstairs.

Marco handed him a fresh beer. 'To the future.'

This was the first time Gianluca had been able to catch up with his cousin since the massive wedding back in Ragusa. They'd played professional football together in their early twenties. Marco had been dropped due to injury; Gianluca had cut his contract at the height of his career and fame to perform the military service expected of a Benedetti male.

He was still feeling the reverberations of that early shot at sporting immortality. Soccer was his country's religion, and for two short years he had been its idol—Rome's favourite son—and nobody let him forget it.

'*Your* future,' he amended, and scanned the room for the bride. Sure enough she was nearby, deep in a huddle with her girlfriends. She was also noticeably pregnant. She saw them and made her way over.

'We were just toasting the Benedetti heir,' Gianluca informed her, kissing each warm cheek she proffered gently.

'That's your son, not mine,' Marco reminded him.

'There aren't going to be any, my friend. So drink up.'

'According to Valentina there will be.'

'You'll fall in love, Gianluca,' said Tina Trigoni, fitting herself into the curve of her husband's arm. She barely came up to his shoulder. 'And before you know it you'll have six sons and six daughters. You'd better,' she added. 'I have no intention of sacrificing my children to the Benedetti legacy.'

'Valentina—' began Marco, but Gianluca gave her a faint smile.

'Glad you've been paying attention, Tina.'

'Although you'll never settle down while you date these bubbleheads.'

He lifted a brow.

'Women with bubbles over their heads—like in the cartoons,' said Tina, making an illustrative gesture. 'Blank bub-bles for other people to fill the words in.'

Gianluca privately acknowledged she wasn't far off the mark. But then he wasn't looking for a mother for his children.

'You've been talking to my mother.'

'God, no. I'm not that brave. You *do* know she thinks a twenty-year-old Sicilian virgin would fill the nursery? I heard her talking to your sisters about it.'

Marco snorted. 'Does your mother know you at all?'

Did his mother know him? Hardly. And that was the point. The Benedettis threw their boys out to be raised like Romulus and Remus in Rome's foundation myth, to be suckled by the she-wolf of the military until they came of age.

His mother had conformed to the Benedetti traditions like all the women who came before her and expected him to do the same.

No, his mother didn't know him—at all.

'Find me a wife then, Tina,' he said derisively. 'A good, plump Sicilian virgin and I'll follow all the customs.'

'Find you a wife and thousands of hopeful women will weep,' Marco observed, swigging his beer.

But Valentina looked interested. 'I don't know about vir-gins—are there any left over the age of twenty-one?'

Completely out of nowhere his mind reverted to a pair of unusual green eyes. There were some, he thought. Once. A long time ago.

'But frankly, Gianluca, I don't know if I should introduce any of my friends to you. It's not as if you're ever serious about a woman.'

'Her friends are queuing up to be introduced,' inserted Marco. 'I'm glad I don't make the kind of money you do.'

'Yes, because then I would have married you for your money,' said Valentina lightly, 'instead of for your charm.' She gave her husband a smart look. 'Besides, I don't think they're entirely after his money, *caro*.'

Gianluca listened to Marco and his wife banter and for a

moment acknowledged that this was what he would miss. All going well, Marco and Tina would grow old together, nurse grandchildren on their laps, reminisce about a life well lived.

In forty years' time... He came to a dead stop. The way he was going he'd be a rich man in an empty castle. He looked past the happy couple and saw only his parents' screaming matches, their empty lives performed on the stage set that was the Palazzo Benedetti. One of the most admired pieces of private real estate in Rome. If only people knew the generations of unhappy women who haunted its corridors.

His own mother had been a stunningly beautiful hot-blooded girl from the hills outside Ragusa. Maria Trigoni had married into the social stratosphere and contorted herself into the role of Roman *principessa*. She had played fitfully at being wife and mother when she hadn't been completely taken up with her lovers or her much-desired role in society.

Her only real loyalty was to her family in the south—the Trigonis. Marco's father was her brother. She would vanish down there for long periods of time. He remembered each one of those disappearances like cuts to his back. The first time it had happened he'd been three and had cried for a week. The second time he'd been six and had been beaten for his tears. When he was ten he'd tried to telephone his mother in Ragusa but she'd refused to take his call.

Privately Gianluca suspected the moment a woman put on the Benedetti wedding tiara she lost a bit of her soul. So sue him—he wouldn't be passing on *that* little tradition.

He swigged his beer, barely tasting it as it went down. He had no intention of settling down, providing an heir to the Benedetti name. It was enough that he'd restored its honour.

Besides, after two years on active service he knew better than most that life was lived in the moment, and at this particular moment he was enjoying a little variety in his life. He knew it irritated his mother, disappointed his grandmother, but as a Benedetti male it was almost expected that he would pursue women in numbers.

The old cliché that there was safety in numbers was true. He had a reputation now for being a bachelor who couldn't be hooked. He played up to it.

As if conjured by the direction of his thoughts a woman stepped out onto the terrace.

She was slender and curvy all at once, and the lights turned her hair platinum.

'There's my cue,' said Gianluca.

'Fast cars and fast women—this is why I refuse to introduce you to my girlfriends,' Tina called mischievously after him.

As he approached, the blonde turned up a flawless face and batted long lashes over her Bambi eyes.

'Come and dance with me, Gianluca.'

'I've got a better idea,' he said, shouldering past her. 'Let's get a drink...' For the life of him he couldn't remember her name.

'Donatella,' she said coldly, in that moment losing the little-girl act.

'Donatella—*si*.' He suspected from her tone that he'd forgotten her name more than once tonight. It wasn't important. She'd only latched on to him because of his name, his reputation.

He slid a hand into his jacket, dragged out his PDA. He'd have a drink, do some work, lose the blonde. But she was a good excuse to put his head back into what mattered—making a deal, setting up the next one, keeping an eye on what the Asia-Pacific markets were doing overnight. Not contemplating what Marco had found seemingly so effortlessly: a good woman. While he, Rome's pre-eminent bachelor, had been stood up by a sexless Australian dragon who clearly didn't know her loss was what's-her-name's gain...

He rifled through his mind for the blonde's name again, gave up, and hit the bar for another drink.

Ava gave her name to the hostess and naturally only drew a blank. Part of her had hoped she would just be waved on in.

'Strawberries,' she whispered.

'Scusi, signorina?'

Ava cleared her throat. 'I believe I'm listed under the name "Strawberries".'

Her mouth felt dry, her skin prickled, and she was sure the couple behind her were finding this hilarious. She closed her eyes briefly to fortify herself. Public humiliation suddenly felt all too close. 'I'm Signor Benedetti's guest.'

Just saying it made this all real, and Ava felt her Dutch courage—a glass of white wine before she left the hotel and two reds downstairs—curdle in her stomach like milk left in the sun.

'Ah, *si.*'

The hostess seemed to find nothing unusual in a woman being listed as a fruit on Gianluca Benedetti's guest list, and the thought made Ava's belly clench a little tighter.

She made her way through a crowd of women in slips and heels and men in Armani before coming to a standstill.

Gianluca Benedetti was lounging like some kind of broad-shouldered Caesar, with his arms thrown across the back of a black leather settee, his powerful shoulders and chest delineated in a form-fitting dark shirt. His high cheekbones, sensuous mouth and uncompromisingly firm jaw gave him the look of one of Michelangelo's marble carvings of male beauty.

Genetics had been so good to him there had to be a price. Spitefully Ava wished she could be around to see it exacted from him. He wasn't alone—as if she had *ever* expected him to be alone. What had she thought? He'd be waiting for her? This was some sort of *date*?

His head was angled negligently to one side for a scantily clad blonde to whisper sweet nothings in his ear.

The blonde, naturally. The stab-your-heart-out heels blonde.

A sick feeling invaded her insides.

She was never going to be that woman.

For a teetering instant Ava was transported to that long-ago reception for her brother's wedding. She had been a socially awkward young woman who just hadn't fitted in with the glamorous, international crowd, watching from the sidelines as Gianluca Benedetti—Italian soccer star and possibly the most desired man on the planet—reclined on a banquette, gesticulating as he talked football with another guy. He'd had two girls wrapped around him like climbing vines, blonde and brunette. The equivalent of gelato flavours for grown men. He hadn't even been paying attention to them.

At the time she had christened them *vines*, but, oh, how she had wanted to be like them. Just for one night to be a sexy, no-consequences girl, in slip and heels, hanging off the hottest guy at the party.

Even as she had struggled to come to terms with the odds of her ever being that kind of girl her eyes had moved over the object of their attention and for the first time in her life she'd been hit by something and hadn't been able to hit back.

The tsunami of feeling that night had carried her past her inhibitions—past the little voice of caution that always asked if this was the right thing to do, if there would be consequences for her actions, the voice of a girl who'd had to look after herself from a very young age. That night she hadn't cared about the consequences.

She had only cared about him.

Having him.

Feeling sick now, she was unable to credit that she had stepped so easily back into the same shoes, that she had learned nothing from her experiences.

Before she could even formulate her next move he was getting up, throwing back those broad shoulders and unexpectedly moving her way. It was so sudden her first instinct was to turn tail and flee, but she wasn't an uncertain girl any more. She could handle this.

Sucking in her tummy, adjusting the line of her dress, she prepared herself for what she would say.

I came but I wish I hadn't. You're a womaniser, a cad and a bounder, and I wish I'd never met you.

He was less than a metre away when she realised he wasn't coming over to her. His hard gaze moved unseeingly over her, as if she were one of the faceless crowd, and Ava realised she wasn't going to have her moment.

He'd issued the invitation but he'd already forgotten about her. She hadn't even made enough impact this morning for her face to register with him.

Her stomach buckled.

She watched him moving easily but inexorably towards the exit, the doors opening and swallowing him up.

Ava only became aware that she was struggling to push her way through the crowd when someone stepped on her foot and she lost a shoe. Pausing to scoop it up, she pushed through the exit doors, then virtually ran outside. She hesitated on the steps leading down into the square, but only to scan desperately for the direction he'd taken.

She gave a start as she caught sight of him, moving out of the darkness across the square.

Shoving it all aside—a lifetime of prudence, plans and protecting herself from men like this one…well, any man really… not to mention leaving her perfectly good A-line coat behind— Ava began to run after him.

CHAPTER FOUR

GIANLUCA HEARD THE FOOTSTEPS, light, fleet heels striking notes on the cobblestones.

He turned around and for a moment they simply looked at one another.

As she began to walk slowly up to him he wondered what had become of his determination never to let life take him by surprise again. His mouth ran dry, his body did what was natural when faced with this much woman. Because, *Dio mio*, she was a sight to make a man glad Adam had had a rib.

She'd obviously gone to some trouble in the transformation department.

It wasn't a stretch to assume it was all for him.

He ran his eye from the erotic promise of her mouth to her decadent bosom and then to the dainty ultra-feminine shoes clasping her feet. No wonder.

The shirt and trousers she'd been hiding beneath this morning hadn't advertised a shape that could only be fully appreciated by an Italian male—generous curves thrown into relief by the accent of her narrow waist.

This was the shape he'd discovered when he'd finally parted her from the puffy blue dress.

She was a walking fantasy if your tastes ran to Gina Lollobrigida.

His did. He'd had a poster of her on the wall of the room he'd kept at his grandparents' villa outside Positano. Part of the pleasure of summer breaks from the military academy he'd been bricked up in by his indifferent parents had been getting back to that house, to his kind old grandparents, but also to Gina.

Almost at once the full force of the past swung in. She wasn't the girl who had lain with him in the grass on the Palatino. That girl had never really existed. And now any trace of her was gone.

As she approached, the low lights of the square illumined her eyes and he glimpsed uncertainty and something else—hopefulness.

But it must have been a trick of the light, because she lifted her chin and her green eyes clashed like an army of the night with his.

There was a dark sort of satisfaction in the knowledge that she had come after him, and it cautioned him to wait and see what she would do.

At the same time he saw what else he'd missed. A huddle of paparazzo across the square. In a second they'd focus in on him, and in this mood the last thing he wanted was a mob of jackals around him.

As excuses went, it wasn't a bad one.

Asserting the cool, dominant masculinity which got him what he wanted in most situations, he stepped up to her, hooked his arm around her waist and told himself this had nothing to do with what he wanted but rather was necessity.

'Scusi, signora,' he murmured, as if apologising for blocking her path, and in the next instant he was kissing her.

He spread his hand at the base of her neck and held her in place, aware this was incredibly intrusive...and undeniably very erotic as she wriggled frantically against him. He clamped his other hand on her wide shifting bottom.

It was still thumping through him exactly who this girl was when he began to enjoy her struggle. He wanted her fists to thump against his chest, her fury at being restrained to come out. *Come on, cara, let's see if you can get away this time.*

He was fiercely turned on, not only by his thoughts but by the feel of her. Her body was so blatantly female every movement of it against his was virtually X-rated. The scent of night-blooming jasmine seemed to be everywhere. His mouth took hers again and then again, until hard and aching he forced himself to release her. All he could see were those bright, astonished green eyes, the curve of her upper lip pinpricked with tiny beads of perspiration, and lower the heaving of her bosom. Instantly he wanted to pull her in tight again, for the press of her warm curvy body that fitted him so perfectly.

In a world of women for whom high heels merely put them on stilts, failing to give them the length in their bodies he needed, he had one in his arms who was built to the perfect scale for a man like him—a little over six feet, with generous hips pressed to cradle his, her breasts soft and full against his chest.

He knew they'd been seen. So he bent his head close to hers. From any sort of distance it was an intimate gesture.

Her green eyes flew to his. Astonishment had given way to fury. It wasn't just in her expression, it was in the aggressive tilt of her body. She was literally seething, and the female pheromones hit him hard and fast, tightening his body into the kind of surging lust he had been careful to keep in check on that long-ago night.

She had been so uncertain. He hadn't wanted to overwhelm her...

But she wasn't that girl any more. She was the woman who had run out on him... And he wanted her any way he could get her right now. Down a dark alley, working up her skirt, tearing her tights, teaching her who was in charge. She didn't run from him. *Ever.*

Gianluca could hear his own harsh breathing.

Why was she pretending not to know him? What had she been doing, walking into the bar dressed like this? What kind of woman was she? The kind who indulged in anonymous couplings with strangers and never looked back? Why in the hell was she back in his life now? What exactly had he walked into?

He glanced in the direction of the paparazzi.

Lust and anger mingled in a disturbing cocktail. What had happened to the cool pragmatic man of his reputation?

He looked down at her, reclaimed the higher ground.

'Scusi, signorina.' The irony in his scraped-down voice was clear, but his code of honour meant he must say it. *'Mi volevi dire nulla di male.'*

He meant her no harm.

No, no harm. He wanted to *kill* her.

Overwhelmed, shocked by the sudden proximity of a big, immeasurably strong male bearing down on her, Ava struggled to make sense of what had just happened even as she instinctively cleaved her body to his.

She should back away now. This was highly imprudent and anything between them couldn't possibly end well. Now was her chance. He wouldn't ask any questions. She was still a stranger to him.

But she hadn't over-exaggerated the memory of the effect of this man on her senses. There had to have been something on that night so long ago that had made her throw all caution to the wind, and now she knew.

She suspected it had something to do with his dark adamantine voice, with that sexy, drawling Italian accent running so softly through everything he said, making her a little bit wild. If she closed her eyes she could feel his mouth trailing the softest butterfly kisses down the centre of her body as if anointing her. Nobody had ever touched her that way before or since.

'Signora?'

Her eyes fluttered open. He was looking down at her with a hot intensity that liquefied her very bones and with something else—something dark and terrifying.

'Signorina,' she answered in a strangled voice. 'Remember, I'm not married.'

He actually reared back slightly, before his eyes narrowed thoughtfully on her.

For a moment neither spoke, and then his half-lidded golden gaze flared out of the darkness at her.

'Can you run in those shoes?'

'S-sorry?' That wasn't what she had expected to hear.

'Those men over there are paparazzo. If they recognise me your photograph will be in all kinds of places you don't want it to be. Can you run in those shoes?'

He didn't wait for her response. He pulled her in against him, one hand on the small of her back, and began walking her fast across the square, back the way they'd come.

Ava knew she should be protesting, or at least asking more questions, but she felt oddly buoyant—furious with him one moment, swept up in excitement the next. And, really, what was she supposed to do when he was just whisking her along with him?

She thought fleetingly of the nearby Trevi Fountain and how in another life she should be there with Bernard right now, pretending to be in an old Hollywood film as he slid the ring she had chosen onto her finger. The thought of how wrong that scenario was on every level floored her. What *had* she been thinking?

Ava glanced up at this man's profile, at the hard lines speaking of an aggressive masculinity that took what it wanted.

Something fierce ripped through her in response and she quickened her pace.

He turned that hard gaze on her. 'You came.'

Ava pushed aside the shiver of premonition, the suspicion he was not just talking about this evening, because all of a sudden he had her hand and they were running.

Too soon they turned a corner and a shiny black limousine glided across the road towards them.

'This is my ride,' he said. 'I prefer to walk on a fine night, but it looks as if we're not in luck, *signorina.*'

He let go of her hand to get the door.

She hung back, hugging herself in the cool spring evening.

'Let me take you where you want to go,' he offered, with an expressive turn of a well-shaped hand, holding the door for her.

And Ava felt herself tumbling through time until she was once more that unhappy girl in a frothy pale blue dress, standing on the steps of a grand *palazzo*, looking in vain for a taxi cab. And he was the beautiful boy with the super-charged ego and five hundred pounds of Ducati growling between his legs, offering her a ride with an attitude of complete confidence.

The confidence had clearly solidified with the years as the dark drawl barely held an enquiry at the end of it. She was a woman. Of course she would dive into his car—no questions asked. Given she had chased after him across the square, joined in when he kissed her, and would still be holding on to his hand like a teenage girl with her first crush if he hadn't released her...he probably had a point.

She had been in limousines before, ferried to and from corporate events that required her to walk the walk. But as she slid across the dark leather seating she recognised this was pure luxury—beyond the expense account of even the multi-million-dollar turnover of her business.

In the street he had been magnetic. Up close in the intimate, quiet confines of the car Ava felt a little overwhelmed by his physicality.

She wished once more she had her coat, aware that her body was on display in this dress, the hem pulling up over her knees. She tugged at it without making much difference.

'I apologise for all the subterfuge.' He sounded so Italian, so *formal*—as if he hadn't kissed her and swept her into his car.

He had pushed back his coat, revealing the hard contours of a supremely fit body. Everything about his clothes screamed money and good taste, and they fitted him with a fidelity that made it impossible for her not to look at him.

Those golden eyes flickered lightly for just a moment over her body, as intimate as any touch, and Ava felt her nipples tightening as heat curled responsively in her pelvis.

It was a shock, wanting him like this. She hadn't expected the pull between them to be this strong. But perhaps it explained one or two things…

'If you give me the name of your hotel I will take you there.'

All of her fears of being exposed, of being disappointed, of losing the specialness of her memory of this man coalesced into one defining moment: *he was going to get rid of her.*

'Or,' he said in a quiet undertone, filling the tense silence, 'we could go on to a quiet place I know first, have a drink, and you can tell me what brings you to Rome.'

He'd said *first*. What came second? Ava tried to ignore the tingling behind her knees, the way it seemed to creep into her thighs. Was he propositioning her? Did he want them to go to her hotel, take their clothes off and…?

Up until this moment she'd agreed with Bernard when he'd told her she just wasn't a passionate woman, and yet here she was, starting up some kind of a sexual fantasy activated by nothing more than a single word: *first*.

'I don't—' she began. *I don't know*, she finished silently. *I don't know how to do this.*

'A drink in a public place. Two civilised people.'

Had he put a faint emphasis on *civilised*?

'Isn't that why you are here…?'

Ava wondered with a sort of horrified fascination if he'd just read her mind…

'To have a drink with me?'

To her continued amazement she felt desire like honey slide through her body. This didn't happen to her. It *never* happened to her. Sexual desire was something she had to *work* on. It never ambushed her like this.

It was a timely reminder that he was a man used to being pursued by women, and she was a woman who had never inspired pursuit in a man.

Most memorably in *this* man.

The heat in her blood suddenly knifed her.

'I won't be sleeping with you tonight.'

He gave her an amused look. 'I wasn't aware I had asked.'

Real embarrassment crawled through her. *She* was the one thinking about sex.

'I wanted to be clear,' she said uncomfortably.

'What if we just have that drink?' He'd leaned forward, clearly to instruct his driver, when something occurred to him. 'Are you hungry?'

Ava shook her head. She didn't think she could stomach a bite.

As he gave instructions to his driver Ava wondered what exactly she thought she was going to accomplish here tonight. She eyed him uncertainly. This entire situation felt illicit and fraught with danger. This was not what a sensible woman did, and beneath the glamorous dress and styled hair she was still at heart a conventional girl in her relationships with men, stand-offish at the best of times. In the hare and the tortoise race she was the tortoise, steadily persevering with a man—specifically with Bernard—until inevitably it all fell apart.

She imagined Gianluca Benedetti's private life moved at supersonic speed, and if anyone ended anything it would be him.

'I apologise,' he said, sitting back, that deep voice made far too seductive by the upper-class Italian accent. 'It wasn't my intention to ignore you tonight.'

No?

'My mind was somewhat preoccupied.'

Snap! 'Yes,' she said, also sitting back, unable to keep some of the derision out of her voice. 'I saw what was occupying it.'

A frown touched his brow.

'The blonde woman who forgot her clothes?' she reminded him.

His expression eased. 'Ah, Donatella, *si.*'

She noticed he made no effort to deny she'd been the source of his preoccupation. Ava tried not to grit her teeth. They weren't on a date. He owed her nothing. She still wanted to hit him.

She didn't really know what she'd been expecting. She suspected it went along the lines of *I remember you. I've never forgotten you. I never got your message...*

'There's something I should tell you.'

'Si?'

'This isn't the first time we've met.'

'Is that so?'

'I don't seem...familiar to you?'

He shrugged.

Ava knew right then that any chance of her making a little joke of it, or him being enchanted or curious, or even maybe a little regretful had evaporated.

'I meet many people. Forgive me if I don't recall your face.'

His tone was reasonable, his words polite—too polite. But the sentiments...they stung...

I don't recall your face. I don't remember lying in the grass on Palatine Hill, cradling you in my arms. I don't remember a single one of the personal confessions you made because, really, it meant nothing to me.

'You really don't remember?' she persevered.

A look of irritation flashed across those hooded eyes.

'No doubt you will tell me.'

Ava knew it was irrational. She knew she had no right to expect something so fleeting, so long ago, to have stayed with him as it had with her. She hadn't realised until that moment how deep she'd been into this fantasy. She really had to stop it now—unless she was keen on full shake-down humiliation.

She stared blindly at the dark window, wishing she hadn't locked herself in such a confined space with him.

'I'm waiting,' he said coldly.

Her gaze was dragged back to his. Why was he looking at her like that? Was she about to break some sort of rule against mentioning illicit encounters in Roman parks? It wasn't as if she'd been stalking him for seven years. She hadn't made a pest of herself. Good grief, she'd done everything possible to avoid thinking about him!

'It's not important,' she said, sounding stiff when what she felt was awkward. 'Let's just forget it.'

He spread those big hands expressively, as if he was actually encouraging her to put him straight. But she wasn't fooled. She had negotiated with sharks before in her professional life.

'Have I read this wrong? You stalk me, pursue me across a public square, and now you hit me with this little confession. What's the angle here, *signorina*?'

The angle? For a moment she struggled to make the connection. She understood the tone. But why was he speaking to her like this?

Ava could feel perspiration prickling along the nape of her neck. She hadn't expected him to be this…intimidating. Where was the sensitive, caring boy she'd found under the swaggering, oh-so-sure-of-himself exterior she'd initially been drawn to? She might have only spent a night with him, but they had *talked*—really talked. She'd said things to him she'd never told another living soul, and at the time it had felt mutual. How had he evolved into this hardened, suspicious man, ready to believe the worst of her at the drop of a hat?

What had happened to him?

'I did not stalk you,' she said woodenly, determined not to show how truly dismayed she was. 'I did not pursue you. Those are not the facts.'

'Come on.' He sat back, looking her over. 'You come to Rico's, dressed like this—'

He gestured at her beautiful frock as if her clothing was an incitement, instead of a fraught choice she had made that afternoon in front of a mirror in a boutique. If the lady assisting hadn't been so genuinely helpful she'd probably be sitting here in a trouser suit.

She was tempted to tell him that far from being a *femme fatale* she was so inept at rolling on stockings she'd ruined two pairs before she'd finished getting ready tonight, and those stockings weren't cheap…

'—on the strength of a flimsy invitation a woman with any common sense and self-esteem would ignore.'

Ava was so busy thinking about the four pieces of cobweb silk she'd left strewn on the bed and the wastage they entailed that she almost missed the impact of the rest of his statement.

The sentiment found its home.

She didn't know where to look. She'd been spot-on back in the bar, when it had occurred to her that he hadn't been serious at all...but she'd taken him very seriously—*too* seriously—and now it was too late to avoid disaster. She'd mistaken the kiss as proof of something. Oh, what was wrong with her? She *always* got social interaction between men and women wrong. Every time.

This was why she'd stuck with Bernard for so long, terrified of what would happen to her out there on the singles scene. She'd been out there once before...when she came back from Rome seven years ago, looking for something approaching what she'd found that night with this man. What she'd got was a guy called Patrick whose sports car and good looks had been her fledgling attempt to put herself out there, to run in the fast lane, and his dating her had been an attempt to slow himself down. She'd discovered a few months into the relationship that he hadn't slowed down at all.

Right now she just wanted out of this car. She needed to run and hide and make sense of this—and then kick herself for being such a fool.

'I didn't issue that invitation. If it was flimsy that's down to you,' she mumbled. 'And you don't need to question my common sense. Right now I'm doing enough of that for the both of us!'

She saw his eyes narrow on her, as if something about this wasn't playing out as he'd expected it to.

When he did speak again it was in a low, silky tone. 'So, where have I gone wrong, *signorina*?'

Just about everywhere! She should be able to laugh about this, but the joke fell flat because it was on her. Right now she knew she was in serious danger of losing it in a major way if she didn't stick to the facts. Cold, hard logic had always been her anchor, her guiding light, and she grasped it now.

'Flimsy invitation or not—' she kept her voice steady '—you *invited* me!' When he didn't react she repeated stubbornly, 'You *invited* me.'

He took out his phone and she watched his thumb move idly over the keypad. He looked so relaxed, as if this entire argument were nothing, and yet his words had been wielded with scalpel-like precision as he took her apart.

'Did you set up the paparazzo?' He didn't even look up.

Ava snorted—she couldn't help it—and his eyes lifted from his phone as if no woman should make such a sound in his vicinity.

Good. She didn't want to be his kind of woman anyhow. 'Do you know what you are? A bully, and a—a playboy, and none of this is fair.'

'Is that so?' His attention had returned to the phone.

'Right now all I'm thinking about is the *hours* I spent getting ready for tonight,' she admitted, wondering why she was even bothering to tell him this—he was much more interested in his phone. 'And I don't have a clue why I did it.'

'To impress me,' he said, as if it were obvious.

Ava's jaw dropped. 'Your ego is astounding!' A blast of anger that demanded she call in a little justice fired up her temper. 'Just you put down that phone and listen to me.'

He lifted his eyes slowly and Ava wished he hadn't. She swallowed—hard—but she'd come a long way in life and she didn't let anyone intimidate her any more.

'I'm not one of those floozies climbing all over you at that bar. Let me give you some facts. Last month I was listed in the top fifty women in business in Australia. It may not mean much to you, *Prince* Benedetti, but it does mean I don't *bar-crawl*, I don't milk men for profit, and I certainly have no idea how you contact a paparazzo.'

'And you are giving me this fascinating glimpse into your life…why?'

With that a great deal of the fight went out of her.

What was she doing? She had a single memory of something wonderful and it was falling apart in front of her eyes. She couldn't even really blame him, because although this man had ripped her blinders off seven years ago the truth was she had sent herself off to live a life devoid of colour, of passion, of sex.

It was a startling realisation, and as if reality had decided to tear down *all* her supports, tension combined with one glass of white wine and three glasses of red on an empty stomach began to swirl and shift in her belly. Everything else was wiped out by the very real knowledge she was probably going to be sick.

'Time to wind this up,' he said, shooting the sleeve on his left arm.

He wanted her to get out. This wasn't his problem. He was just a man to whom everything came easily, and she was a woman for whom nothing had come without hard work. She gathered up her handbag.

'Come,' he said brusquely. 'Give me the address of your hotel and I will see you home.'

Ava ignored him and grappled with the door. The flash of impatience she'd heard in his voice had her retaliating as she struggled out, 'Why bother? You didn't last time.'

It was an unfair thing to say, but she was past being fair, and it would have made for a great exit line—but she ruined it by toppling straight onto her hands and knees in the gutter.

Could it possibly get worse? Swearing under her breath, she clambered to her feet, hopping about as she whisked off her heels. She'd walk in her stockinged feet. She might as well— she'd just laddered her last pair anyway.

She was plodding down the street, not sure where she was going, when she heard him call out in that deep, resonant voice.

'Evie!'

She didn't even turn around, wondering who the hell Evie

was. Right now she just wanted to put as many blocks as she could between them.

Oh, why was everything so hard for her? Other women went on dates, were romanced, kissed, cuddled and adored. Other women came to Rome and had adventures. She felt pretty sure all of those women didn't end the night walking the streets in their stockinged feet.

Blearily she rummaged in her bag for the hotel's card she'd picked up on her way out this morning. All she needed to do was find someone and present it, and get some directions. How hard could it be?

She gave an *oomph* as she almost toppled over a stone bench that had somehow leapt into her path, but an unyielding male hand closed around her elbow and fluidly turned her into his arms.

'Stop it—let me go!' she huffed, pushing against his chest, aware mostly of the heat of his body, the delicious scent of him, and her own giddy reaction as she tried to free herself. She turned this way and that until she realised he wasn't holding on to her, just trying to steady her. Why did she need steadying?

She heard him say, '*Dio*, you're drunk.'

It wasn't an accusation…more an observation.

She lifted her chin to sling back a clever reply—something along the lines of, *I'd have to be to go anywhere with you…*

Instead she gazed owlishly up at him.

'I will drive you back to your hotel,' he informed her in a tight voice, but somehow he didn't seem angry any more.

Ava wanted to argue, but she already knew she was in no condition to make a fuss.

'Where to, *Principe*?'

His driver, Bruno, addressed Gianluca calmly over the roof of the limo, as if ferrying drunken sick women around the city nightspots was a regular occurrence.

Good question.

A sensible man would find out where she was staying, do the right thing and not look back.

Si, a sensible man… He'd just bounded out of the car and charged after her, so clearly he didn't qualify.

He had not behaved sensibly from the moment he'd put the Jota into a screaming U-turn this morning. No, it was long past time to assert his much-vaunted judgement.

He leaned down to find out where she was staying.

To his surprise she appeared to be asleep. He gave her a gentle shake. Her head fell forward.

Bene! Drunk. Blind drunk.

Swearing under his breath, he noticed her right hand was clutching something. When he prised open her fingers he found some crumpled euros and an embossed white card.

She was offering him money?

A cab—of course… It all clicked into place. She'd thought he would just bundle her into a cab? In her condition?

Pulling back on his first thought to wake her up and get this sorted out, he retrieved the card.

The Excelsior.

Nice hotel. Not far from here.

Being as careful as he could, he gently shifted her into a more comfortable position. Her mouth hung slightly open and she was breathing softly. For the first time the tension had left her face. She looked as if butter wouldn't melt in her mouth. She looked like a woman who *didn't* go to bars to pick up men and drink so much she passed out. She looked, in short, like the kind of woman who needed looking after.

He pitied the poor *bastardo* who ended up with that job.

Then he noticed other things. There were holes in the knees of her stockings. Her dress was thin. She must have been cold out on the street. Not questioning his actions, he shrugged out of his coat and laid the heavy silk-lined jacket over her.

Unexpectedly she pulled her head back and opened her eyes, green and swimming. She seemed to try and focus. For a moment neither of them spoke, and then she dropped her head again and made a sound that reminded him a little of a hog rooting for truffles. He was so astonished he smiled.

Straightening up, Gianluca slid the hotel card into his back pocket.

'*Casa mia,*' he said to Bruno. Home.

CHAPTER FIVE

'WAKE UP, SLEEPING BEAUTY.'

A deep, sexy male voice nudged her out of her dream.

Who says I'm not a passionate woman? Ava thought happily as the landscape of his face enlarged, each delicious detail communicating itself to her—the olive perfection of his skin, the line of his sensuous lips, eyes so golden they blistered like a flame over black heat until all she could see was the darker rim of his iris, like an eclipse of the sun. Everything was dark and warm and...*real*.

He was kissing her. The feel of his lips coaxing hers so confidently had all the hormones in her body popping like seeds coming to the surface of the earth after a long winter. She strained towards him and long fingers tangled in her hair as he murmured against her lips, *'Cosi dolce, cosi dolce, mi baci bella.'*

So romantic...so enticing...so real...

She lurched to full consciousness. Her eyes flew open and fixed on the living, breathing version of the dream she had entertained too many times over the years. All two hundred pounds of prime female fantasy.

'You!'

'Yes, me, *bella*. Who did you think you were kissing? Or do we all blur after a while?'

What on earth was he talking about?

Lifting her hands to his chest, she gave him an almighty

shove. But he was fixed over her, his expression nowhere near as friendly as his mouth had been.

'Get off me, you—'

Ava wasn't sure what to call him, but the solid weight of all that hard muscle under the flat of her hands, the appealing masculine scent of him curling around her, and her mouth still tingling like an electrical storm after his kiss made her protests sound a little feeble to her ears.

He clearly thought so too. He gave her an intriguing appraisal from her bed-head hair, to her raccoon eyes, to her bare shoulders.

Bare shoulders.

Ava clapped a hand to her chest. She was naked. Holy hell! She was too well-endowed to be going around without a little stitching and support. She wriggled. No, not naked. She definitely had her knickers on. Vaguely she remembered flinging her clothes off. She was pretty sure no one else had been involved.

'Get off,' she slung at him again.

'I like you better when you're unconscious,' he commented. But before she could process that he had sprung up with a lithe, muscular grace she could only envy and was heading for the door.

Ava struggled to sit up and keep the sheet gathered modestly under her arms. Her eyes widened slightly, because for a moment there she thought she'd glimpsed a distinct bulge in those jeans.

A band tightened around her skull and she winced.

'Where are you going?' she groaned.

'It's a new day, Ava. Get dressed.'

And with that smooth-as-silk instruction he was gone.

Ava stared at the door he'd shut behind him and then down at her own long shape, wrapped in a white sheet like a mermaid. Instinctively her fingertips caressed the fabric—a thread count so high it felt like water on her bare skin. For a moment her mind went fuzzy again, and she felt the softness of his breath mingling with hers, the solid weight of him under the press of her hands and the new knowledge that he was every bit as susceptible as she.

Come back, her libido pleaded.

She slapped a hand to her head. What had got into her? Her hormones had led her into all this trouble and she was still letting them run riot!

The pulsing behind her eyes gave an extra punch, as if to remind her of the evils of giving in to rogue impulses, and she lowered her head carefully back down onto the pillow. It felt like a brick.

Get dressed, Ava... He could go to hell...

Ava... Get dressed Ava.

Ava.

She almost fell out of bed. He knew.

He needed a cold shower.

Gianluca stood under the pulsing jets in the wet room, massaging out the tension bunching in the tendons behind his neck.

Ava Lord.

Not *Evie*—Ava.

For seven years when he'd thought of her—and it was about time he acknowledged he *had* thought of her—it had been as Evie.

It had been one night, years ago. How could he be expected to get her name right? But he had never known her real name. Somehow he'd misheard, and she hadn't corrected him, and right now *that* was the sticking point for him. Had it been so anonymous for her she didn't need names? And why was that little detail bothering him? A better question was why did his gut muscles clench when he remembered rolling over and finding her gone?

He'd been twenty-two at the time, had what he'd imagined was success, in the form of a media frenzy around his soccer career, and girls had been climbing down drainpipes to perform for him. He'd been an *idiota* plenty of times in those early years when it came to women, and he'd been pretty jaded by the time Evie…*Ava* dropped into his lap.

It had been different, though. *She* had been different. She'd had attitude even then—giving him directions when he was cruising the Ducati downtown, fussing and complaining. He'd humoured her and pretended to get lost. He'd thought he'd enjoy watching her lose it…but she hadn't.

Instead she'd lost her edge and grown curious about his city, and then excited when he took her to the Forum, where she'd wanted to know the entire history of the place. He'd found himself having to compete with monuments and long-dead historical figures for her attention.

She'd made him compete. She'd forced from him what other girls had never demanded—to be entertained. By the time they'd reached the top of Palatine Hill she'd had him in the palm of her hand.

He actually hadn't planned anything when they'd sunk down into the grass. She'd talked a lot, he remembered, and he'd found he didn't mind listening. He might have said a few things himself, and when she'd begun to cry he had kissed her, because her tears had felt real. It probably wouldn't have gone beyond that…but she had smelled incredible, and tasted so sweet, felt warm and soft. The minute he'd slid his hands under the boned bodice of her fairy-tale dress and felt the warm satin weight of her breasts, her nipples pushing up against his palms, there had been no going back.

He had known she wasn't like any girl he'd ever met. He had known there would be a messy aftermath. He had known he was inviting a thousand complications into his clear-cut life but he'd dived in anyway.

Evie, Evie, Evie. *Ava.*

What he hadn't known was that she'd cut and run before he could learn another detail, and within minutes of waking to an empty bed he'd received the phone call that had changed his life.

He was still shouldering those changes.

What he also hadn't known then was that seven years later he'd be woken at 6:00 a.m. by another phone call, this time from his cousin Alessia, to tell him her husband's sister was in Rome. She was refusing point-blank to come to them. He was to bring her with him this weekend.

'Her name is Ava Lord and she's staying at the Excelsior. Josh has been ringing and ringing, but her phone's switched off.'

This had been followed by another phone call from his mother. 'You *must* pick up this girl, Gianluca. Alessia tells me she refuses to come to us. We were not kind to her at Alessia's wedding, and I'm afraid it's influencing her decision-making. I feel it's my fault.'

Gianluca killed the water jets and, shaking his cropped dark hair free of water, padded from the wet room, dragging a towel over his shoulders.

Ava Lord.

Alessia only had to say her name and he knew what he'd done.

He'd gone and slept with the groom's sister!

He shaved and dressed rapidly, punching his arms into his shirt, swearing under his breath. Going into his room earlier this morning he'd intended to confront her. But that had been his first mistake.

He'd found her lying in the middle of his bed, twisted in a sheet that did nothing *not* to remind him of how lush her curves were, making it pretty obvious that she was naked under the sheet.

Her thick, lustrous hair had been spread about and one arm flung out, as if to showcase the curve of shoulder, breast and hip. It was a ratio of numbers that would make a mathematician weep.

She had shifted, and the full impact of her made-for-sin body had been outlined in fine white Egyptian cotton. All the blood in his body that hadn't already headed that way had surged to his groin.

Madre di Dio.

How was he supposed to conduct any sort of conversation with her and not think about sex?

Irritated, he'd hit the controls for the window shutters and a wave of morning light had splashed over the bed. He'd intended the harsh light of day to take the edge off her sensual display.

'Come on—wake up.'

He had reached down to shake her but his hand had hovered over her bare shoulder. He'd tried to find a portion of her body he could touch with impunity, but she seemed to be made up entirely of erogenous zones. He had known if he touched any part of her it would be soft and pliant and far too female, and his self-control would be history...

Cursing under his breath, he had struggled to peel his mind off the rise and fall of her chest.

'Wake up, Sleeping Beauty.'

She'd murmured something and his gaze had been drawn away from the sheet and due north, like a compass, to that strawberry of a mouth, as luscious as any of her curves. Sultry green eyes had gleamed behind slowly lifting lashes.

She'd absolutely killed him.

God help him, he'd wanted another taste of the soft pink fullness of her lips, the heat of her mouth, the explosive re-action in the kiss they had shared last night. His ungoverned imagination had moved on, taking the sheet down slowly. He would shape the heaviness of her breasts with his hands and feast on nipples he remembered amazingly clearly as being the same strawberry colour as her mouth...and when she was wet and wanting, begging him to come into her, he would push himself deep inside her, fill her hard and...

She'd given a sigh, gazing dreamily up at him as if await-ing his pleasure. There had been only one thing for it under the circumstances.

He'd leant down and found her lips with his, and that kiss in the *piazza* last night had been pushed aside by the sweetness of this one. Her mouth had been as luscious as he'd remembered, and just like last night she had responded. This time there had been no fury in her—just sleepy, soft sensuality.

Even half asleep she had kissed a man as if her heart and soul were involved, and he had found himself tangling his hands in her thick, silky hair until...

'You!'

He had drawn back and seen the shock and accusation in her eyes. As if she'd had no idea who she was kissing. As if she responded to every man who put his arms around her, drew her close, put his mouth on hers with the same *incredible* abandon.

Dio mio, he told himself now, as he put his hand to the door. It wasn't jealousy of other men that had driven him from that room this morning into a cold, cold shower. It was a matter of good taste.

This was not some woman he'd just picked up last night. There would be no indiscriminate coupling. Not now that he knew her identity.

She was his guest. She was Alessia's sister-in-law. She was the one woman in Rome he definitely *wouldn't* be sleeping with.

This time he made sure he knocked before shoving open the door. He didn't know what he expected—at the very least a woman dressed. Her hair would be better neatly combed away into that ugly knot she'd been wearing yesterday—before all of this got out of hand.

Instead she was sitting in the middle of the bed, legs tucked under her, wearing the sheet.

Still wearing the sheet.

Naked.

'Santa Maria,' he snarled. 'For the sake of decency, will you put some clothes on?'

Her head jerked around and for a moment she looked almost shocked. But it must have been a trick of the light because those green eyes instantly narrowed and she yanked at the sheet, winding it more securely under her soft, pale arms.

Bene. That was exactly what he wanted. Her covered up. Except if anything the gesture only exaggerated the spill of flesh beneath her fine collarbones and made her more of a feast for his male senses.

He hadn't realised until this moment how incredibly appealing a voluptuous woman could look in nothing but a bed-sheet. He'd clearly been sleeping with far too many skinny girls. She was every inch Venus emerging from the foam. A goddess of love and sex and the secrets of the flesh. If she went about in nothing else but a sheet there would be riots on the streets of Rome…

'*That's* what you've got to say to me?' She sounded incredulous.

He tore his thoughts away from her bountiful cleavage and told himself he needed to tackle this rationally—and for that to happen ideally certain things needed to occur. He needed another cold shower and she would need to be dressed. But, frankly, he didn't have time.

He folded his arms. 'I've got plenty to say to you, Signorina Lord,' he said heavily. 'Given your lack of modesty, we'll get started now. Does your brother know you're here?'

She blinked at him. Clearly it wasn't what she'd expected him to say.

'My brother?'

'*Si*—the brother you so cleverly omitted to mention.'

She shook her head. 'Why are you interested in my brother?'

'I suspect he would have been interested in me seven years ago, when I deflowered his sister in a public park.'

The look on her face was priceless.

She clearly understood nothing. His position, hers, how everything had now taken on a different complexion.

'I am the head of the Benedetti family. You are a de facto member of that family by marriage. I hold responsibility for your safety while you're here in my city.'

It was a perfectly reasonable thing to say. Gianluca waited for her response. A little feminine reserve would go a long way at this moment. She would ask for his assistance and he would give it.

She gave him an incredulous look. 'You are *kidding*?'

Gianluca knew in that moment this was going to be a long morning.

'I rarely...*kid*.'

'Then I'd kindly ask you to keep your nose out of my private business. You most certainly are not responsible for me—and nor, may I add, is my brother.'

'In point of fact,' he responded with bite, 'I *am* responsible for your brother. I employ him.'

'You do not,' she asserted confidently. 'Josh runs a vineyard in Ragusa.'

'*Si*—on my land in Sicily.'

Ava frowned. This wasn't the picture Josh had painted in their rare phone calls. She had thought he was doing well, that he was his own man and the vineyard he owned was thriving. In point of fact when she'd last talked to him a few days ago he'd used the start of the harvest as an excuse not to see her.

'I'm not any happier about this than you, Signora Lord. A day never starts well when my mother feels the need to phone me.'

'*Signorina,*' she reminded him—then wished she hadn't, given the now speculative look on his face.

'*Signorina,*' he said, disturbingly softly.

'Yes, well...I've heard about how close Italian men are to their mothers,' she bustled on crisply.

'We speak three times a year: Easter, Christmas and her birthday.'

His eyes moved lazily over her and Ava shifted a little.

'This morning will make it four—because of *you, signorina.*'

'I'm bringing mother and son together,' she responded dryly. 'I'm doing you a service.'

He ignored her. 'According to the women of my family, with whom I make it my practice not to get involved,' he added with wry emphasis, 'you refuse to see your brother because you feel they have offended you in some way.'

She didn't miss the way he made it sound doubtful that any-one had offended her, as if his precious family couldn't pos-sibly have done anything to hurt her...

Ava's temper was rekindled. 'What's it got to do with them?'

'Apparently they feel responsible for some unhappiness you experienced at your brother's wedding all those years ago.'

You. You are responsible for my unhappiness!

Ava sucked in a breath, aware she had been far too close to blurting that sentiment out. Where on earth had it come from? Surely she didn't believe that? But she was very afraid she did, and it was motivating her frustration with him.

Almost helplessly she silently willed him to mention the real issue, which was their long-ago night together, so she could dismiss it out loud as unimportant and all in the past.

'It's not their business,' she said mulishly when she realised that—just like a man—he had said all he was going to say.

'You can discuss it with them,' he said.

'I'm certainly not discussing it with *you!*'

'*Bene.* I have no interest in your varied sex life. I am, how-ever, the man who will be sending you south this afternoon.'

What varied sex life? He'd clearly confused her with one of his bimbos.

She watched him scoop up her dress, which she'd so em-barrassingly thrown onto the floor in her drunken state last night. He shook it out and tossed it to her.

Ava watched in horror as he picked up her bra—all pretty black lace filigree, but substantial enough to support her—and dangled it in front of her.

She snatched it from him, narrowing her eyes at him. He probably had a pile of these—souvenirs from all the other women who had passed through this room. Oh, if only the walls could talk—if only she could find that pile, wrench open the door and point out his stash and confront him with his rampant promiscuity...

Gianluca said calmly, 'Once you are dressed we will talk about this.'

What? No suggestive comments? No questions as to why she'd seen fit to strip herself in the middle of the night...? No interest on his part in her being naked...?

Ava was suddenly aware that what she was feeling was fast approaching disappointment. It was completely inappropriate and she veered her thoughts in the other direction. She really should have got dressed some time ago, instead of sitting here mulling over what he knew and didn't know.

It was clear he knew *everything.*

CHAPTER SIX

'DID YOU HEAR ME?' he repeated impatiently. 'Dress yourself and we will talk.'

'Just a minute.' She gathered the sheet around her, as if another layer might give her the requisite dignity she felt she was presently lacking. 'What have you said to your mother about me?'

'My mother?' He rubbed the back of his neck, drawing into prominence an impressive bicep.

'Yes—the woman who gave birth to you,' she snapped impatiently, convinced he was just showing off his incredible body to taunt her. 'Or did you spring fully formed from the head of Zeus? I wouldn't be surprised...' She muttered the last.

'You really want to discuss my mother?'

No, she wanted to run a hundred miles in the other direction from his mother!

She had experience in facing down corporate sharks in boardrooms when a lesser woman would be knock-kneed to enter, but Maria Benedetti—La Principessa—had looked down her patrician nose at Ava seven years ago, as if the Lord family were somehow not good enough for the Benedettis.

God knew what she would say about this situation—her precious firstborn son standing over her, fully dressed, groomed, every inch the cool upper-class Italian male, and she in her knickers, wrapped in a sheet, at a complete disadvantage after a drunken night on the tiles.

If only she hadn't rung Josh. But she'd been so unhappy when she had first landed in Rome she'd been desperate to hear a familiar voice. He'd been so standoffish she'd turned off her phone, and now his wife wanted to stick her nose in...

'Signorina Lord?' he rapped out impatiently.

'What?'

'Get dressed.'

'No. I want to know what you said to her!' Ava was aware her voice had risen rather shrilly and knew it could be ascribed to panic.

He scrubbed his jaw with the heel of his hand. 'I won't be mentioning our little encounter, if that's what concerns you.'

'I didn't mean that.'

Unaccountably she wondered why he wouldn't mention it. What exactly was wrong with her?

'Anyway, there was no "encounter", as you call it,' she grumbled. 'Unless you had your way with me while I was unconscious.'

An electric silence greeted her suggestion.

'Not that I'm accusing you of anything,' she amended, beginning to feel a little uncomfortable.

The silence lengthened.

'All right—forget it,' she muttered, not sure where to look.

'I can assure you that did *not* happen,' he breathed, as if she had been offensive.

'I was joking.'

'You are naked in my bed,' he said with precision. 'I call that an encounter.'

'You must be slipping.'

He gave her such a long look she began to feel a little flushed.

'Indeed I must be,' he said at last. Restlessly Ava tucked the sheet a little more firmly under her arms.

'What do you call last night?' he asked, still watching her closely. 'A typical Friday night?'

A typical Friday night for her was working after everyone

else had gone home, a glass of her favourite wine and an episode of *Poirot*.

She would just *die* if he knew that.

'I call it being drunk and heartsick,' she said haughtily.

'Drunk, yes. But, flattering as I may find it, I doubt you are still holding a candle for me, *cara*.'

Once you've ridden a giant rollercoaster, the small ones for ever after seem tame.

Longing welled up at that thought and flooded her.

'And if you are,' he said, in the same stroking voice, 'you need to let it go.'

From nowhere, resentment went off in her body like a rocket.

'Heartsick over my boyfriend, you pig—not you!'

His expression grew taut again. 'You will refrain from calling me names.'

Ava felt the heat rush to her face and knew she was revealing too much about her feelings.

'I apologise,' she said stiffly, before adding, 'But you provoked me.'

One dark eyebrow lifted, as if this couldn't possibly be the case. 'Where is this boyfriend?' he said, clearly sceptical.

'None of your business.'

'He lets you out at night on your own? To sit at bars and drink?'

'I do *not* sit at bars and drink! And what do you mean—*lets* me? I'm a grown woman. I can do what I like.'

'He is not Italian, then?'

'Who?'

'The *boyfriend*.' He said it as if she'd just made Bernard up.

Hitching up the sheet, she strode off the bed like a ship in full sail and headed for her handbag, sitting on the armchair under the window.

Furiously she rummaged in it with one hand.

'What are you doing now?'

The low rumble of amusement in his voice was not helping

her temper. She wrenched open her bag and dug around until she located her phone.

'Here. This. Look.'

She held up a recent image of Bernard's pleasant settled face as he'd sat opposite her in a famous Sydney harbourside restaurant. She liked this picture because in it he looked like everything she'd needed him to be but often was not: solid, reliable, dependable.

'My boyfriend,' she said, as if producing a rabbit out of a hat.

Gianluca glanced seemingly without interest at the image.

'You could do better.'

'Pardon me?'

'He has no love for you or you would not be here on your own. If you were *my* woman you would know better than to behave as you did last night.'

Ava tried not to imagine exactly what being his woman would involve, but her instinctive, *completely un-PC* response must have shown, because there was something all too like a male lion surveying his pride of females about the way he was looking at her.

That did it.

She wasn't having this. She really wasn't. Not from him.

'Are you *serious*?' Her voice rose to an unbecoming level. '*Your* woman? What does that even mean? And you know nothing—*nothing*—about my relationship with Bernard!'

'Bernard?' he repeated. The amusement lurking in those golden eyes almost undid her completely.

'Yes, Bernard.' To her horror tears sprang up behind her eyes. She couldn't bear it if this man made fun of her—of her sad, mixed-up reasons for that particular relationship. It was all such a mess. 'For your information we came to Rome to get engaged, but we broke up! Oh, what would *you* know about relationships anyway? You use women and throw them away.'

'*Cosa?*'

'You heard me. You're a—a rake.'

'My English is usually very good,' he said smoothly, 'but are you comparing me to a garden implement?'

And just like that the fight went out of her. He wasn't taking any of this seriously and she was making an idiot of herself—again. Ava shook her head and quietly put Bernard back in her bag. She scanned the floor for her shoes.

'I need to go,' she said. 'Just forget all of this even happened.'

Gianluca didn't respond, and when she glanced up she realised why. He had taken his phone out.

Nice.

Thoroughly disillusioned and miserable with herself, Ava dropped to her knees and reached under the bed, feeling for her shoes. Belatedly she realised she was sticking her most ample asset into prominence—but really what did it matter at this late stage?

Gianluca Benedetti was a gorgeous man with a habit of beautiful women, and she wasn't his type…at all. And, frankly, when it came down to it he wasn't very nice…

'Ava.'

The way he said her name sent shivers through her. It was really inconvenient. Still, it wasn't as if she'd be hearing her name on his lips for much longer.

'What?' she asked ungraciously, hooking her head out from under the bed.

He was looking at her bottom.

Ava almost hit her head on the bedframe in her haste to get herself vertical.

'*Bella*, what are you doing?'

Was it her imagination or was his voice pitched lower than earlier? And why was he calling her beautiful?

'My shoes—they're missing.'

'You don't say? Come here.' He beckoned to her with that well-shaped hand.

When she hesitated he looked faintly exasperated, as if waiting around wasn't something he was used to.

'*Adesso, cara.* I have something to show you.'

He was clearly not used to waiting around. Most women probably leapt to attention when they heard His Master's Voice, she thought witheringly.

He extended his phone to her.

It was one of those ultra-sleek not long on the market models. Under normal circumstances Ava would have practically salivated.

Instead she almost dropped it.

Her stomach bottomed out.

A man and a woman engaged in a clinch on a cobblestoned square at night.

It would have been romantic but for the identity of the couple.

'It's too far away. You can't see the faces,' she said hopefully, her voice airless.

Gianluca scrolled to the next image.

Himself—amazingly photogenic—it seemed, along with everything else—up close in a smooch with a woman whose eyes were closed and who had a look on her face Ava hadn't even known she could produce. She looked as if she was swooning, and perhaps she was. She looked like everything her ex Bernard had accused her of not being.

A woman carried away by passion.

'Is that me?' She lightly touched the screen with her index finger.

The image didn't dissolve. It was real.

'Welcome to my life,' he informed her tightly.

For some reason she could feel him regarding her closely.

'Public property.'

Ava snatched the phone off him and began to scroll frantically through the shots. In two of them it was clearly her. Then she shrieked, 'Oh, God—I look so fat!'

'That's all you have to say?'

'It's all right for you.' She eyed him mutinously. 'You're not wearing shiny fabric and being shot at an unfortunate angle.'

Gianluca retrieved the phone. 'You look fine. And that's not the issue.'

She looked *fine*?

Last night was the best she'd ever looked…and he thought she'd looked fine. That didn't leave her with far to go this morning, with her bed hair and smudged make-up.

'You need to leave Rome—now—and I'll need to know where you are.'

Still contemplating the fact that her round behind looked at least a size bigger in that photograph, and that the entire world was going to be looking at it and making comparisons with every skinny-minnie model he'd ever dated, she was a little slow to pick up on what he was saying.

'Leave Rome?' she repeated, then focussed. 'Leave Rome! Why?'

'Because more photographs will be taken of you. Information will be sourced. You will be a five-minute wonder.'

'Information? What information?'

'Your name, your origin, what you do, who you are. Run-of-the-mill for me, but not so much for you, *si*? So you go to Ragusa for a few days and this dies down.'

'Like hell!'

'There is also the small issue of my future wife,' he said under his breath as he scrolled through the messages on his phone.

Ava's head whipped around.

He glanced up and had the grace to look marginally uncomfortable.

'It's a joke, Ava.' He made a gesture. *'Non e importante.'*

Ava forgot all about her behind being shown around the globe for the world's media to lampoon as she felt something fragile and new sprouting inside her wither and collapse.

'You're engaged and you *cracked onto me*?' She couldn't keep the feeling out of her voice.

'Cracked?' He pocketed the phone and made one of those extravagant Latin gestures of incomprehension with his hand.

'Tried it on…made overtures…you know—*cracked*.'

'I'm not engaged yet,' was his cool response.

'Semantics,' she shot back, her entire stomach free-falling. 'Oh, what a piece of work you are. Well, you can stuff it.' She began looking for her shoes again, this time throwing things around—cushions, the throw on the armchair. She would have liked to have flung the chair at him.

His voice wrapped round her like a strong arm. 'I wasn't the one trawling for sex, *cara*.'

Ava stopped thrashing about. In point of fact her arms went spaghetti limp and her head jerked round. 'Excuse me?'

He was watching her with that cool, Italian sex appeal some women probably found irresistible.

'Look, I understand you're broken-hearted or whatever—'

Again with the scepticism. 'Let's go with whatever,' she retorted.

'But you weren't looking for Prince Charming last night,' he finished with brutal candour.

'And guess what?' she snapped back. 'I didn't find him!'

In that moment she hated him so much that if she'd had something to hand she really would have thrown it at him.

He was *engaged*—and who knew how many women had been under his bridge in the last seven years?

Whereas she'd had exactly three. *Three!* Three men under her bridge. She'd kept her bridge nice. He probably had a toll on his. Thousandth woman through gets a bottle of Bollinger and an engagement ring. How dared he call her morality into question?

'I'm not going anywhere, bud. This is your problem. You caused this. You were the one who kissed *me*.'

'I will remind you that it was you who chased after me like a demented banshee across that square. I wasn't given much choice after that little performance.'

Great—so now he'd kissed her because he'd had to.

'And now, *signorina*, because of your activities last night we're front page on Rome's leading gossip sheet. Which means my PR people will be spinning this because you're family, and so, like a good member of the extended Benedetti family, you're going to be where the rest of us are this weekend.'

'What do you mean? I'm not a member of the Benedetti family!'

'You, madam, are going to Ragusa.'

'I bloody well am not! I've booked a driving tour of Tuscany.'

A romantic trip she was now doing all on her own.

He laughed. He actually laughed.

She didn't think. She reacted. Overcome by a surge of feeling far beyond what his reaction warranted, she lunged at him.

He caught her arm easily and dislodged the sheet. Ava gasped and, unable to stop the slippage, jammed her breasts up against his chest, effectively imprisoning the sheet but giving him a full body imprint. Outrage dissolved as she suddenly found herself in a very precarious position.

He felt hard and hot and...interested. Yes, definitely considerable interest on his part. A lightning flash of sexual heat shot up her body in response and her nipples sprang out like little pink missile launchers. If she'd wanted his attention she now had it.

She was appalled by how quickly this entire situation had got out of hand. She couldn't believe she'd physically attacked him. Couldn't believe anything about this mess and drama was turning her on—and, unexpectedly, him. Oh, yes, his arousal was unambiguous against her belly and she could feel the tremor in his body.

'Let me go!' she squeaked, unable to look up because they were so close. She didn't trust him or herself. She'd been forced to address the base of his throat, where the skin was golden and dark hairs curled invitingly, and she fought the urge to touch him there too.

To her surprise he did as she asked and let her go. Ava grabbed at the sheet, hauling it into place and sitting down heavily on the bed, feeling very much at a disadvantage. She couldn't fight her corner like this. Where was her dignity?

She pulled clumsily at the bedsheet toga, making sure everything was securely in place.

'I'm not a member of your family,' she reiterated. 'You can't force me to go anywhere.'

She glanced warily at him and discovered he was watching her broodingly. For a moment she thought he was actually considering that she might be right. Instead of feeling triumphant, Ava experienced a trickle of uneasiness as she realised after this morning she would probably never see him again.

'Besides,' she said, trying to ignore that feeling, 'how will you explain kissing a member of your sainted family, Mr Spin Doctor?'

'It was a friendly peck, blown up as something else by the nature of photography,' he said with amazing cool, his golden eyes screened by dense black lashes. 'We had both dined with friends and I was escorting you back to the *palazzo*.'

Her mouth fell open slightly. Damn, he was good. It must be practice. Her eyes narrowed like a cat's.

'You are, naturally, staying with me, and today we travel south and join the rest of the family for my mother's birthday celebration at the weekend.'

Ava swallowed. Another Benedetti clan gathering. Another opportunity for her to feel like a spare wheel. She really, *really* didn't want to go.

'Is your fiancée going to be there?'

He actually looked discomfited. 'There is no fiancée,' he said, with the air of a man being made to suffer.

To Ava's amazement colour scored those ridiculously high cheekbones.

'There will be a lot of people at Ragusa next weekend. Those photographs will be discussed. Nobody who knows me is going to believe the story. We will be the object of some speculation.'

'That bothers you, does it?' she said stiffly, thinking of the

blonde with almost no clothes on last night. He might as well
have said, *I don't want my friends and family to meet you and
think we're a couple.*

He pushed his fingers restlessly through his thick hair. '*Dio*,
it is the custom in my family for the eldest son to marry and
produce the next generation. It is the reason I never—*never*—
bring a woman with me to Ragusa. This—' he indicated her
and the rumpled bed '—and me arriving with you in tow is
going to cause trouble.'

'Don't worry,' she said stonily, staring past him, her heart
pounding, because she'd thought she was long past being the
girl who didn't make the grade, 'your mother *hates* me. She'll
probably put strychnine in my water and then all the speculation will stop.'

There was a loaded silence.

'Besides, I'm not coming. If I don't turn up there won't be
a problem, will there?'

Ava told herself the petulance in her voice was merely the
end effect of a week in which she'd been on the wrong end of
the stick with not one man but two. Two men who were clearly
happy to put their own comfort before her own. As if her feelings weren't worth even a little consideration. As if she didn't
have feelings at all.

Was that why Bernard had thought it fine to break up with
her over the phone?

As for Italy's Natural Wonder here—she'd seen him in action last night and was under no illusions as to the kind of
women he dated or how he treated them. She should be glad
she knew how he saw her—a mistake from the past, one he'd
been lumbered with and was now doing the best he could
to limit damage to his reputation, to his comfort. She knew
all about that. Her father had given her early lessons in just
how disposable she could be, always putting his needs first,
constantly cancelling access visits, until eventually he didn't
bother to show up at all.

She needed to keep that in mind. That way she wouldn't be

doing anything silly—as she had last night, when she'd kissed him, or this morning, when she'd kissed him again… Really, she had to stop the kissing!

But none of it explained why this man putting himself first should actually *hurt* her, when Bernard's actions had done nothing more than upset her travel plans. It was baffling.

He was nothing to her.

CHAPTER SEVEN

GIANLUCA STOOD AT THE open window, watching as Ava climbed into a taxi. She was sneaking out again—after he'd given her specific instructions to get herself dressed and join him downstairs.

Very few people defied him, and despite the trouble she had caused he couldn't help admiring her determination.

She'd pinched his coat, which was far too big for her, and with her hair standing up on end and without her shoes she looked like a woman fleeing a morning-after gone awry. It briefly crossed his mind that this was how it must have been all those years ago, when he'd been oblivious upstairs in his bed. His smile deserted him.

He remembered waking and reaching for something—someone—who was no longer there. When he'd realised she was gone, leaving nothing—no note, no contact, no name, just shoes—instead of the relief which had been his usual reaction at that age, when a girl from the night before vanished back into the ether from which she came, possessive instincts he hadn't known he harboured had ramped up and he'd been out of that bed, pulling on his clothes, determined to track her down.

Then the phone call had come...

His father's body had been discovered and taken to the hospital. He had driven there instead, and by the time he'd got around to looking there had been no trace of Cinderella...

Just the shoes she'd left behind.

Those shoes.

Red, with complicated straps.

Si. His expression grew taut and some of the volatility he worked hard to contain tightened his hands on the window frame. It was the shoes he had recognised yesterday on some subliminal level. Not the girl. She had been hidden under layers no self-respecting Roman woman would venture outside in. So completely without style, without manners, and with her femininity clearly of no interest to her. No man would have looked twice at her.

Yet he had.

Which made him suspect something else was at work here.

The cold, rational diagnostics he'd relied on to build one of the most successful trading firms in the world were clearly not standing up to the bone-deep traditions he'd been raised with.

Benedettis didn't show emotion. They put duty above personal desire, gave service to the state. But the customs and currency of his mother's volatile Sicilian family—peasants from the mountains, bandits and priests—meant that when you took a woman's virginity it meant something. Deep down at some primal male level where it was probably best to keep it buried, it had created a bond. In former days he would probably have married her.

Gianluca cleared his throat. Fortunately they were not living in former days. Besides, he was Rome's pre-eminent bachelor. He'd once made the throwaway comment that he'd marry when George Clooney cashed in his single days and it had appeared in print a few days later, out of context, cementing his desirability for a certain ambitious class of woman.

Although Ava seemed not to realise he was a catch. She seemed to find it imperative to run away from him whenever the opportunity afforded itself. He found a growl had risen in the back of his throat as he watched her taxi drive away.

There was no other woman who had left his bed so fast or so anonymously.

Run from him.

Even now something almost primitive drummed inside his skull. She would leave when he told her she could leave. It was a feudal notion, but he wasn't going to step away from his very strong masculine instinct to hold what was his.

In the back of the taxi cab Ava stopped fuming and began rummaging in her bag for her phone.

It was just a bit of harmless research, she told herself, as she tapped his name into a search engine. She wasn't exactly being nosy—just protecting her interests.

She scanned his many entries, wondering where the football-playing career had gone. It seemed to have been swallowed up by venture capital projects, leveraged buyouts, takeovers, private equity deals. All of it involving the kind of financial acumen and strategic planning she hadn't factored in to her admittedly somewhat dated picture of this man.

The family business, she told herself sternly. That was all. He was a Benedetti. Finance was in his blood. The family had always owned banks. Benedetti International, however, was a relatively new entity, and it already dominated the markets. Which meant he must be doing something right.

A little thrown by her discoveries, she pressed on images and the small screen flickered to life with pictures. Her thumb only trembling slightly, she clicked her way through Gianluca Benedetti at film premieres, parties, the FIFA World Cup, a polo match in Bahrain, as a guest at a royal wedding. In nearly every single photo a beautiful girl in a slinky dress was glued to his side.

He certainly didn't seem to have a type. Tall, short, reed-slim, curvy... Her mouth tightened. True to form, *female* seemed to cover it for him. And in numbers.

True, he didn't seem to be serious about any of them—not that it mattered. She would guess that when he finally got around to it, Gianluca Benedetti would do the whole romantic proposal/engagement thing properly—if only because he liked to be the best at everything.

The woman would get the full package. He wouldn't need pointers. He'd probably fly one of those leggy heiresses to the Bahamas, whip out a diamond the size of a rock and serenade her with a string orchestra.

Whatever...

Ava snapped her phone shut. What a woman *wouldn't* get from him was an assurance that he wouldn't follow the next fast-moving skirt in the other direction...

Although dullness hadn't stopped Bernard from doing exactly that!

Nice, safe Bernard. Her go-to boyfriend. When people asked *How is your life going?* they didn't mean your business being listed on the stock market—well done. Your employees have reported high enjoyment stats from their job—good on you. You own a place with a harbourside view outright, on your own—fabulous! What people really meant when they talked about 'your life' were your relationships. Everyone wanted you to be in a couple of sorts. To have what they had. Otherwise you stood out too much, you attracted attention, you were *different*. Ava had had enough of being different growing up to last her a lifetime.

Socially, a partner was important, too. You couldn't just turn up to functions on your own.

Meeting Bernard at twenty-nine had been a huge release from those demands. Instead of turning up with a different man on her arm every time—or, worse, alone—she'd had Bernard. People had begun to remember his name. They'd been invited to more intimate functions. People had referred to them as a couple, and gradually they'd become one.

It had suited them both—professionally and personally. If the initial spark between them had never been anything more than a fizzle, they still had a working friendship to fall back on.

But deep down she'd always known that if he left her—unlike when her father had walked out—she wouldn't be heartbroken.

Perhaps the proposal in Rome had been her get-out-of-jail-free card. Perhaps deep down she had known it would push Bernard to make the decision they both knew had been on the cards. It wasn't as if their intimate life had even existed for the last six months. Now she knew why. He'd been going elsewhere, to another woman for *passion*. But she'd hardly noticed—and what on earth did *that* say about her?

The same thing Bernard had said. She just wasn't a passionate woman.

But she did want a little romance. In her longing for that she'd forgotten what her relationship with Bernard had been all about. Practicalities. Practicalities *she* had put in place.

So for five minutes she'd imagined herself into a relationship that didn't exist. A proposal by the Trevi Fountain. A driving tour of Tuscany. Perhaps they'd find an old villa, come back to Italy every summer and restore it... She might even wear a button-front cotton dress and forget to put on her shoes, stomp grapes between her toes... All clichés she'd gathered from films and books about finding oneself in *bella Italia*.

With Bernard?

He had never liked her in a skirt—said a woman with her hips was better off in trousers. She'd been forever buttoning up her shirts for him when he'd said her cleavage made her look like a barmaid. Moreover, *he* wouldn't have been able to restore anything—not with his dust allergy—and as for stomping grapes with his bare feet...well, she couldn't actually remember a time when she had seen him without shoes and socks outside of bed. No, he *did* wear his socks to bed...

The thought depressed her so much Ava sat up a little straighter. Unexpectedly she thought of Gianluca Benedetti's long, well-shaped feet, their smooth olive skin, the way her smaller feet had tangled with his in the white silk sheets.

No, no, *no*.

Grappling with the window, she wound it down and cool air hit her hot face.

She looked out into the busy morning traffic and told herself to do what her deadbeat dad, on the scant occasions she had spent with him as a small girl, had always told her to do when she asked why he didn't live with them anymore and whether it was her fault: toughen up, not ask stupid questions and then she wouldn't get a stupid answer.

Ava closed her eyes. No. No more stupid questions. The sooner she put mileage between herself and His Highness the better.

Safe in her hotel suite, Ava showered and, still slightly damp in her robe, began transferring her clothes into her suitcase, aware she had a scarce half hour before she was expected to be out of there. She was convinced she was doing the right thing. So why was her conscience niggling? Josh didn't really want to see her. He didn't need her. He'd made that plain enough seven years ago and followed it up with such limited contact she no longer phoned him even on his birthday, only sent cards.

Seven years ago in this very city she'd told him she thought he was making a mistake, marrying so young when he had his whole life before him. He in turn had told her the reason he'd fled Australia at the age of eighteen was to get out from under her thumb, and that he had no intention of taking her advice. Furthermore, she knew nothing about love, because the only thing she cared about was her bank balance. If she ever found a man who stuck around it would probably be for her money. She was going to end up rich, disappointed and alone.

Ava noisily zipped up her suitcase. There was a sharp rap on her door. Room Service with her late breakfast.

'It's open!' she called out, her voice a little shaky as she pushed aside the painful memory.

'You should be more careful, *bella*. This is not a safe city for a woman on her own.'

Gianluca strolled in before she could so much as move to slam the door in his face.

'Good to see you've packed—but you need to put some clothes on.'

Ava squeaked her dismay.

'How much luggage do you have? There's not much room in the Jota.'

'I am not going anywhere with you,' she protested, even as she drank in the scent of him so close to her, absorbed the strength of those shoulders clad simply in an open-necked shirt and a sports jacket. How did he manage to look so stylish and at the same time supremely masculine? What was wrong with her that everything female in her leapt at the sight of him? She folded her arms across her traitorous breasts, well aware, given how sensitive they were to him, that everything would be on display.

'Come now.' He smiled down at her, pinched her chin. 'No more games, Ava. We go now.'

She wrenched her chin free, shocked by the intimacy the gesture implied. It made her shriller than she needed to be. 'This isn't a game, Benedetti. I have a car booked. I intend to see Tuscany.'

'Monday.'

'Sorry?'

'I will fly you there myself. Next Monday. But first you must do the right thing, *si*? Join the family.'

'Your family. Not mine.' Something lurched in her chest, because she'd met the Benedettis and they had looked down their noses at her.

'It depends,' he said, brushing the tangle of damp hair out of her eyes as if he had every right to touch her.

Ava tried to avoid his hand but he hooked an unruly lock over her ear.

'Your brother is in some financial difficulty with the vineyard.'

Ava stopped dodging his hand. Now he had her attention.

'What are you talking about?'

'Perhaps his marriage is not in good shape because of this?'

Ava frowned, trying not to enjoy his fingers tangling in her hair, trying to focus on what he was saying about Josh.

She really ought to make him stop.

'Your presence might be—what is it called?—the elixir they need.'

'His marriage is in trouble?'

His hand dropped away from her hair and he picked up her suitcase.

Ava digested this startling news and told herself she wasn't thinking *I told him so. I warned him. I was right.* Josh needed her.

She touched her hair where Gianluca's fingers had played so intrusively.

Suddenly Tuscany didn't seem at all important.

'Why should I believe you?'

He merely hefted her suitcase off the bed.

'Go and put some clothes on, *cara.* We leave in ten minutes.'

He was waiting outside, leaning against the same low-slung machine she'd seen him in the other day.

He looked as if he'd stepped out of the pages of *GQ*—six and a half feet of Italian cool.

Swinging her handbag over her shoulder, she told herself to get moving and to stop ogling him. He was a gorgeous man, but if he knew the power he had over her he was sure to use it against her.

'Well, let's get this over with,' she said.

Gianluca simply stared.

In receipt of his loaded silence, Ava lifted a hand uneasily to her hair, neatly pulled back into what she'd thought was a fetching ponytail.

'What are you staring at?'

'Why are you dressed as a man?'

Convinced she hadn't heard him right, Ava repeated, 'Dressed as—?'

A man?

He was frowning at her. She'd heard him right. Her skin began to feel tight all over and then to prickle.

He thought she looked like a man?

Gianluca Benedetti's expression was a study in masculine perplexity even as Ava wished the ground would swallow her up.

Not looked like a man, she reminded herself. *Dressed as a man. It's not the same thing.*

'It cannot be that you are now a lesbian?'

In any other situation Ava would have reminded herself that she celebrated human sexuality in all its richness and diversity. Right now, under the scrutiny of the most aggressively heterosexual man she had ever known—moreover a man who had kissed her last night and this morning with such a devastating effect on her senses she was still under its influence— she felt as if he'd slapped her.

With a handful of words he'd scraped off the layers of confidence she'd painted on over the years and exposed the sensitive young girl who'd never known her place in the world until she'd toughened up and gone out and made a place for herself. This man had been born gorgeous, entitled and rich. A man who never doubted his place in the world.

'Yes,' she said, tilting up her chin, 'that's exactly what I am. A card-carrying, definitely-no-men-on-board lesbian. Can we go now? The sooner we start out the quicker this will be over.'

He opened her door.

'I can do that myself, you know,' she snapped, and slid inside.

He shut the door with a click.

'I can do that too,' she muttered, stuffing her bag down at her feet and adjusting the seatbelt.

He was beside her but made no move to start the car.

'I thought we were in a hurry,' she said stiffly. She hated that she now felt self-conscious in her tailored black pants and high-necked white silk blouse. There was nothing wrong with her clothes. They were practical.

She eyed his bespoke jacket, the crisp pale green shirt that somehow clung to his broad chest and muscle-packed waist and abdomen as if it had been ironed on, the faithful fit of those dark jeans to his long, powerful legs. He looked as if he'd stepped off the catwalk at Milan, and she had a flash of the sort of woman who would stride off that catwalk with him. Elegant, racehorse-thin, not afraid of colour.

Ava plucked at her sleeve. At least her silk blouse wouldn't crease, and there was absolutely nothing wrong with the black trousers. They gave the illusion of a flat tummy and reduced the impact of her round derrière. She had twelve pairs hanging up in her closet at home. A woman who wasn't reed-thin needed to downplay her lumps and bumps.

He had the body of a Roman athlete, fresh from killing something in the arena. Whatever he wore was going to look good.

Not that she was paying particular attention to how good he looked. No, she was just settling accounts in her head. There were all sorts of reasons she preferred black and white to… Why weren't they going anywhere?

'Why aren't we going anywhere?' she demanded, refusing to look at him.

'I have offended you,' he said unexpectedly.

'Don't be ridiculous,' she muttered.

'I am not accustomed to women wearing trousers.' He spoke carefully, as if choosing his words. 'I shouldn't have implied you lack femininity because of your wardrobe choices.'

Ava felt her stomach hollow out.

'You presuppose I care what you think.'

But she did care. She suddenly wished she'd put on a skirt. But she didn't own a skirt.

She turned her head and immediately wished she hadn't, because he was so close. Too close. She could see where he'd shaved this morning, see the indent of his upper lip, and had a sudden, shocking longing to press her mouth to it.

'I know you were trying to insult me, but it's water off a duck's back,' she informed him, wrenching her attention off his ridiculously sensuous lips. 'What I am about to say will come as a shock to you, as I suspect no woman has ever told you the truth.'

'You could be right.'

'But I'm not afraid of the truth. I like to face things head-on.'

'Go on,' he encouraged, almost gently.

A little thrown, Ava gathered herself together. He wasn't being nice to her. He was just lying low to get her to attack him and then he'd swing in with something insulting that made her feel...made her feel...

'The truth is you're just a handsome face with a lot of money and a habit of control, so women let you get away with murder. I haven't and you don't like that.'

'Is that so?' He was smiling at her as if he saw right through her.

Ava looked away, folding her arms. 'That's so,' she said, and wondered why she didn't sound sure.

CHAPTER EIGHT

GIANLUCA SLOTTED THE Jota in at the circular entrance and leapt out with an energy and purpose that mocked her indecision.

Ava trembled, frustrated by her own complicated desires as she climbed out of the car.

'Why have you brought me back here?'

'It is my home.'

'I understand that,' she said with exaggerated patience, but he was already taking the steps, leaving her standing by the car.

He wasn't giving her any time to think. Ava said something rude under her breath and took off after him.

In the vast entrance hall she was vaguely conscious of the black and white parquet underfoot, the grand shallow staircase ahead. But only because Gianluca was on his way up it.

'Benedetti!'

He didn't respond.

'I demand you answer me!' she shouted, and her voice echoed around them. She jumped, startled.

He lifted his hands in a gesture of male impatience.

'Must we have theatrics every time you fail to notice the obvious?'

Ava was on the verge of informing him that she'd never indulged in theatrics in her life. She was a calm, measured woman and she never shouted... She was only shouting now because he was—which was when she realised he was on the move again. She hurried upstairs after him. Why were they going upstairs? His bedroom was upstairs. *Lots* of bedrooms were upstairs.

'What is obvious?' she demanded, her voice only quavering slightly. 'This is *not* the airport.'

'No, it is my home.'

Ava narrowed her eyes on him. 'At the risk of pointing out more of the obvious, your home is *not* an airport! How do we get from here to Ragusa?'

He stopped so suddenly she ran right into the back of him. Hot, hard and sturdy.

His hand shot out to steady her and excitement flowered inside her as he smiled wolfishly down at her. She wrenched her arm away, glaring at him.

She held her breath.

'Helicopter,' he said simply.

Helicopter? Once they reached the roof Ava was unable to take her eyes off the rotating blades.

She couldn't go up in that.

Moreover, what sort of man had a helipad on the roof of his house?

If you could call this palace a home.

She'd only glimpsed it this morning, in her run for safety, but in the broad light of day, following Gianluca's confident stride up the stairs, along a brightly lit hall, passing an enfilade of windows, she realised it was indeed close to being a palace—in the centre of Rome. No wonder he behaved as if he'd invented the word entitlement.

And here on the roof, with the wind stirring up from the rotorblades roping her hair around her neck, Ava was struck by the view of the city.

Somehow seeing the *palazzo* in broad daylight made it all too real.

But it was the rotating blades that held her in thrall.

'I'm not climbing into *that*!' she shouted as Gianluca gestured for her to follow.

'Too late, *dolcezza*.' His resonant voice was easily heard above the *whup-whup* of the rotors. 'We have an appointment in Ragusa and this is the quickest way to get us there.'

Ragusa. Yes. Of course that was what she wanted too. But he didn't have to make it sound as if he wanted this to be over.

The noise of the rotors put paid to her thoughts as he secured her harness belt. She told herself for the nth time that thousands of people went up in helicopters every year and nobody fell out, and then she had the unexpected thought that he might not be coming with her.

He leaned in. 'Ava, you don't have a problem with heights, do you?'

She shook her head vigorously, finding she didn't have a voice for the words *Don't leave me*, which were sticking in her throat.

'Motion sickness?'

'No,' she choked.

He gave her a long, measured look and then surprisingly lifted one of his hands and stroked her hair.

'Bene.'

She couldn't bear him to be kind to her or she wouldn't be able to do this. Didn't he understand all of this was difficult for her? Being with him after seven years, knowing at the other end of this flight was his family and social scrutiny—something she'd never been able to bear?

Didn't he understand her anger was the only thing holding her together? A welling of hot, harsh fury spouted through her as if in answer to her need, and as he moved to bring the helmet down over her head she thrust her hands up to take it from him.

'I'm not incapable, you know. I *do* ride a bike.'

The pilot beside her let rip a laugh and said something to Gianluca in Italian, too fast and distorted by the noise for her to follow. She imagined it wasn't complimentary.

What she did understand was that he was giving up the controls to Gianluca.

'You're flying this thing?'

'A man should try everything once, *cara*.'

She tried not to enjoy the moment. She really did. But the moment they were in the air her heart almost lifted out of her chest.

Down below lay Rome in all its glory, and beside her, his hands steady on the controls, the scion of one of Rome's most storied families. Beside *her*, ordinary Ava Lord, to whom nothing remarkable ever happened that she hadn't planned, organised and executed herself.

'It's good, yes?'

He was looking at her with those mesmerising eyes, his wide, sensual mouth warm with amusement.

She didn't know what to say without sounding stupid, over-awed, thrilled beyond measure. She felt like a little girl at the top of a rollercoaster.

He gave a husky, appreciative laugh at her baffled expression.

She had to say something. 'When did you learn to fly one of these?'

'In the Marina Militare.'

She hadn't seen that coming. 'You were in the Navy?'

'Si.'

'But—' she began, and then stopped. *What? He can't have a life beyond what you allow him, Ava?*

Had she really spent the last seven years with Gianluca Benedetti sitting in a little box marked 'mine'?

'Before or after you were everyone's favourite soccer star?'

'I played football for five minutes professionally, *cara*. It's hardly been my life.'

'I imagined—' She broke off again, because telling him what had been going on in her head for seven years would be far too personal and revealing.

'Ah, *si*, that imagination of yours.'

He reached out unexpectedly and took her hand. His thumb rubbed over her palm, sending sparks shooting up her arm.

'What *have* you been imagining, Ava?'

'Nothing,' she said immediately. *Everything.* All those women! 'I don't have an imagination.' What did he know about her imagination anyway? That had been a long time ago, when she was a little girl who didn't know life was never going to live up to what was in her head.

So she'd faced reality—had to, really—until one day people had begun labelling her as humourless and dull. Always the new girl at school who never got the joke, never made friends, who wore the same unfashionable clothes day after day. It hadn't mattered. She'd been too busy with part-time work, chasing up Josh over his homework and keeping a roof over their heads to worry much about her popularity as a teenager.

She snatched her hand back and he let her go.

'How long were you in the Navy?' she demanded.

'Two years. I flew an Apache on three tours of Afghanistan.'

'You flew in a war zone?'

'*Si*, in a rescue squadron.'

Ava forgot all about her own discomfort. How had she not known this about him?

'Why did you—?'

'Join up? I like to fly,' he said, with a shrug of those wide shoulders. 'I like to challenge myself. The Navy has the best equipment in the world. I wanted to try it out.'

'That's the worst reason I've ever heard for joining the armed forces.'

'There are worse reasons.' He looked grim for a moment. 'Besides, what would I know? I was just a dumb footballer.'

'I doubt you were ever a dumb anything,' she replied acerbically, 'given what you've achieved. And you're not yet thirty-one!'

'I didn't say I wasn't a *lucky* dumb footballer.'

Ava tried not to stare at him. 'So you joined your father's business after all?'

He shot another look at her. 'You do remember a great deal, for a woman who wants to forget, *cara*.'

She could feel herself colouring—and she *never* blushed.

'I didn't join anything,' he continued blandly. 'By the time I got out of the Navy the Benedetti private banking firm was defunct.'

'But you had connections?' she persevered.

He laughed, but it sounded flat, and Ava felt obscurely guilty for bringing up the subject.

'I came out with nothing but a Maserati, which I sold. I invested in a friend's boat-building business…moved on up from there. Venture capital is high-risk, and most people don't have the stomach for it.'

She knew that. She was one of those people.

'I take it you do?' Ava's mouth was dry as paper.

'What do you think?'

Her eyes were glued to his hard-jawed profile. Suddenly so much made sense about him—the big, physically tough body that didn't fit a man who wheeled and dealed on the money markets, the flintiness she sensed at his core.

He had been to war, and it seemed things hadn't quite worked out the way she had imagined. He wasn't just some spoiled boy who had been handed his life on a platter.

Ava didn't quite know what to say. She settled on a very weak, 'You *have* been busy.'

He chuckled.

'What's so funny?'

'Your expression. It's getting hard, isn't it, *cara*?'

'Pardon?'

'Finding reasons to dislike me.'

'I haven't said I dislike you.' It was supposed to come out as a statement, but it sounded far too uncertain for her liking.

'We should look at doing something together.'

Still sorting through her feelings, she found a highly intimate recollection of the things they had done together flash unexpectedly to mind. Ava felt her face heating.

'Do something?' she repeated airlessly.

He gave her a smile, as if he knew where her thoughts had gone.

'*Si.* You're clearly very talented.'

'I am?' *Oh, good grief, he's not talking about sex, Ava!*

'The Lord Trust Company—a full-service brokerage firm, founded four years ago.' He grinned and her stomach flip-flopped. 'You've got some loyal clients.'

Business. He's talking about your business, she reminded herself. She frowned. 'You've researched me?'

'I'm always looking for new companies to add to my portfolio. If you want to expand.'

She had almost forgotten this was a man who prowled the stock markets of the world like a ravening beast.

For the first time in many years she couldn't have given a damn about her business. Her gaze dropped to his hands, so capable on the controls, and she flashed to an image of those hands so dark against her milk-pale flesh. Of herself arching into them, so utterly uninhibited she couldn't quite believe she had ever been that girl.

'Ava?'

She blinked at him, bemused, and his answering slow smile had her heart doing a *pah-pound, pah-pound* rhythm.

'When did you research me?' she uttered, with a suddenly dry mouth.

The slow smile increased. 'This morning over coffee.'

'Funny—I did the same with you.' Her gaze dropped help-lessly to his mouth.

'What did you discover?'

'Enough. But somehow not everything…'

His smile faded.

'Benedetti International is a far-flung enterprise, *cara*, even I have trouble keeping track of our interests.'

She highly doubted that—Gianluca Benedetti struck her as a man who knew what he was about at all times and she would be a fool to forget it. But it was a shock to realise she hadn't been thinking about business at all. Her thoughts had been entirely taken up with his private life, which really was none of her affair. She gave him an anxious look, thrown by her own response to him.

The mountainous terrain below was giving way to the coast, and Ava risked craning her neck to see it rather than confront where her thoughts were leading her.

The cliffs were stupendous, falling away into the water. Towns clung to the sides. She had seen picture postcards of the Amalfi Coast, but hadn't quite believed it was this pretty.

'It's beautiful, *si*?' he said softly.

'Yes, beautiful. I wish—' She stopped and his eyes captured hers.

'What do you wish, *cara*?' he asked, like the devil after her soul.

What did she wish? Too many things—and they came over her in a rush.

To be the girl she had been on that long-ago night—softer, willing to share her feelings for the first and only time in her life, instead of being constantly on her guard against being attacked, ridiculed, exposed...let down.

Her early years had taught her too many harsh lessons about showing vulnerability. About people taking advantage, not living up to their promises. She had applied those lessons to business and they had steered her well.

But she had also applied them when she'd climbed out of his bed seven years ago, and right at this minute she wished with all her heart that she had made a different decision that morning—that against all odds something could have come of that night.

Even more fancifully she wished for this to be a romantic trip away together, at the beginning of their relationship, when everything was full of possibility—and for him not to be a playboy, spoilt by too many women, and herself not to be a woman who prided herself on playing it safe.

It was foolish, and her wistful expression was undoubtedly

telling him everything she didn't want him to know, and yet she couldn't stop the feelings from rushing in…

It was a shock when his expression unexpectedly hardened with determination.

With a quiet, 'Hold on,' Gianluca angled the helicopter and without warning they swooped inland.

At first she thought he was giving her a better look at the town clinging to the cliffs, and then she realised they were dropping down just below the mountain peak. Too low. Much, much too low.

Ava's pulse began to surge.

Directly beneath them was a helipad above a grove of pines.

With a sense of inevitability she realised she was going to get her wish. They were going to land.

CHAPTER NINE

THE ENGINE CUT and the rotors slowed and whirred to a gradual halt. Gianluca whipped off his helmet, tackling his harness with the same economy of movement.

'What's going on? What are we doing here?'

'I've got a meeting I should have taken in Rome today,' he responded, as if he were stating the obvious. 'I've decided to take it in Positano.'

Ava's mouth fell open. 'You're *what*?'

But he was already leaping out, leaving her sitting harnessed to her seat. He'd done this on purpose. She felt sure he did *everything* on purpose to undermine and confuse her. Frustrated, Ava began tugging at the belts, getting herself hopelessly tangled up.

She knew she was overreacting, but her own longings suddenly felt entirely too dangerous in this new situation.

'This was *not* what we agreed to,' she erupted as he came alongside her, his capable hands taking hold of the harness.

'Relax, *cara*,' he advised. She wasn't sure if he meant over being kidnapped or to make it easier for him to unhook her.

'The hard part's over.'

A little stunned that he'd recognised her fear of heights when she thought she'd hidden it so well, Ava held still long enough for him to unhook and free her. She wanted to slap away the hand he offered, but falling flat on her face wouldn't be a good look, so she took the assistance he proffered and concentrated on disembarking.

She wasn't sure how it happened, but in stepping down she pitched forward. He caught her, and she was suddenly very conscious of her soft breasts pressed up against his hard chest. A memory of the last time they'd been this close flamed to mind. His hands settled on her hips. Her legs did a little wobble.

'The hotel here is owned by a friend of mine,' he was saying.

She tried to wriggle free, but it only provided friction between them. Friction she didn't need! His mouth felt far too close to her ear.

'We relax, enjoy the amenities, you tell me about yourself and we go from there, *si*?'

Go where? What was he talking about? She trembled as one of his hands drifted to her waist, tightened.

He drew back, his eyes intent on hers.

'Seven years is a long time, Ava. We have a lot of catching up to do.'

Ava's heart stuttered to a halt.

What was he saying? Was he saying what she thought he was saying?

She gave a little gasp. What was he doing with his hand? Somehow her shirt had come a little adrift of her pants and his rough, broad fingers slid underneath. She felt the firm press of his large dry palm shaping the indent of her waist and the flare of her hip under her waistband. Lightly stroking. His long fingers stretched higher over her ribs and Ava caught her breath, her breasts swelling, her nipples tightening with anticipation.

'Stop it!' she hissed. But she wasn't quite sure who she was addressing, and there was a suspicious lack of force behind it.

Two men were coming up the slope to the helipad from the gardens, their voices intruding, and with a powerfully intent look Gianluca released her and turned away to deal with them as if nothing out of the ordinary had happened. When *everything* had just happened to her.

She heard him issuing instructions in Italian, something about their luggage, and realised she was still just standing where he'd left her, with her shirt adrift, gazing stupidly after him.

'Oh, good grief,' she muttered, and rapidly began stuffing the hem of her shirt into her waistband, mortified. What was she *doing*, letting him feel her up like a teenage girl? Where was her dignity?

She walked up to him and stopped a good metre away, arms folded. 'What do you think you're playing at, Benedetti?'

He looked her up and down, as if everything about her amused him, but she saw he was noticing where a little of her shirt still hung loose. She tucked it in fast with her free hand, aware she hadn't exactly been fighting him off.

'Glad to see the flight hasn't dented your charm, *cara*,' he observed with a bit of a smile. 'But next time you throw yourself into my arms give me fair warning and I'll try to arrange it so we don't have an audience.'

Ava's gaze shot to the men dealing with their luggage.

'I did not throw myself at you,' she hissed.

But he was already heading down the steps.

'I thought the idea was to get from A to B as efficiently as possible,' she called after him.

'This is most efficient. I conduct a little business; you enjoy a little down time; we keep each other company.'

'Company?'

He shrugged those wide shoulders.

'My brother—' she began, hurrying to keep up with his long strides.

'Twenty-four hours ago you cared so little for your brother you refused to answer his phone calls.'

Ava stared at his back in horror. 'How do you know that?'

'What is more, you never had any intention of seeing him. I cannot help but wonder, *cara*, if this sudden overwhelming need to rush to his side has more to do with spending time with *me*.'

Ava almost choked.

'And, as I have already told you...' He stopped and she almost ran into his back. As he turned around she backed up. 'I am most happy to accommodate you.'

'Accommodate me?'

'My English...' He shrugged, but she caught the amusement lurking in those golden eyes.

His English was bloody perfect, she thought, feeling hot all over.

She followed him out of the hot sun into a southern coastal garden, with a wide, sandy path underfoot, narrowing as it wound down through the trees. But Ava was too focussed on the lean, muscular physique of the man in front of her to pay it much mind.

From his attitude he clearly expected her to fall into line with his wants and needs. *Keep him company!* She eyed his lean, muscular physique resentfully.

He could find all the company he wanted, but it wouldn't be hers.

The minute she was in possession of her belongings again she would make arrangements and be out of here so fast he wouldn't know what had hit his privileged behind.

Unnecessarily her eyes were drawn to that behind... Incredibly taut, it made a masterpiece of those fitted dark jeans.

'I don't know why you ever imagined I would let you get away with this,' she called after him.

He continued walking down the path, moving with that easy, wide-shouldered grace she could only envy. She hobbled behind him.

'Bringing me here like some sort of concubine.'

'You really need to get this imagination of yours under control, *cara*. I have a meeting.'

'And I've already told you I don't have an imagination.

You're unbelievable. *You* have a meeting. What about *my* meetings, my life? That's all on hold!'

'You are on holiday.' He turned around and Ava tried not to be swayed by his warm eyes, his half tilted mouth. He looked completely relaxed, and she felt…she felt…

'Yes, my *holiday*.' She seized on the concept, veering away from those inconvenient longings. 'And you're such a Neanderthal you think you can just hijack it on a whim.'

'That is the second time you have compared me to our early ancestors.' He suddenly looked like a big cat, deciding whether to take a swipe.

Ava felt a little uneasy. She hadn't actually thought he was paying attention to her insults. How worried should she be that he was keeping score?

'I wonder why,' she shot back.

'I have a contemporary outlook,' he said simply.

'Yes, that's apparent,' she snapped.

He raised an enquiring brow.

'You behave like…like a Roman Caesar. You have run roughshod over my wishes from the moment we met. You critique my clothes, as if as a woman I should only be dressing for a man!'

'It is clear you do not,' he responded, resuming his stride.

Ava ignored him. 'You behaved last night as if I'd committed a crime by informing you that we were previously—' she cast about for a suitable neutral description for a night she had never forgotten and came up with '—acquainted.'

'I was naturally cautious.'

She snorted. 'I'm sure you encounter predatory women all the time. How disappointing for you that I'm not one of them!'

'Yes, we would possibly have less trouble now.'

Brought up short, Ava frowned and halted. She wasn't sure if there was an insult in that comment, or a backhanded compliment, but it was clear as day which sort of woman he'd prefer.

'I feel sorry for you,' she slung at his broad back. 'Never knowing if a woman is interested in you or your bank balance.'

He shrugged.

'And you're promiscuous. You lecture me, but *you*, Benedetti, are a playboy of the worst kind. You treat women like playthings. That sort of thinking went out in the Seventies, along with Sean Connery playing James Bond.'

'Connery continued to play Bond into the Eighties,' he inserted dryly as they approached a large gate cut like a keyhole into the stone wall. He gave her a shockingly charismatic smile over his shoulder. 'But do go on. I would like to hear some more of your opinion of me.'

He thought this was funny!

'No, you wouldn't. What you want is to be praised. All men do.'

'*All* men? This would come from your vast experience of my sex, *cara*?'

Ava looked around for a rock. She needed one heavy enough to cause some damage when she threw it at his head.

He turned, folding his arms across his chest. 'Tell me about all these men.'

Ava suddenly wished she'd slept with a hundred men. She wished she had put the last seven years to better use. Right at this very moment it seemed as if bed-hopping would have been a far better utilisation of her time than attaching herself to a dull, self-effacing man and building a business with a national reputation.

She gritted her teeth.

'I don't know how you dare to stand in judgement on my sex life when your own is nothing to brag about.'

He gestured with one hand, as if he didn't have a clue what she was talking about. 'What is this bragging?'

Ava didn't know. She didn't really know anything about him other than how he made her feel. Out of her depth, out of bounds, a little crazy.

Passionate.

Her thoughts came to a juddering halt. *Look at me*, she thought, a little light-headedly. *Burning up like a firework ever since he came strolling back into my life...*

'It's obvious you're proud of your reputation,' she rattled on, desperately holding on to her anger. Because this man might have strolled in, but he would also stroll out. Guys like Benedetti didn't stick.

'You think sleeping with hundreds of women makes you such a man, when really all it makes you is cheap.'

He had been watching her with a slight smile, his big shoulders relaxed, as if she were providing some form of impromptu entertainment, but her last words had hit their mark, because the smile got lost and his jaw hardened.

Right—good. Ava realised she had unconsciously balled up her hands into fists.

'Yes, cheap—to be had by anyone if she hitches up her skirt and bats her eyelashes at you.'

He closed the space between them and Ava had to force herself to hold her ground. The scent of him took up an assault on her hormones, making her a little dizzy.

'As I recall you did both those things last night,' he said in a low voice, his eyes moving over her face, 'and yet still I refused you.'

His words went through her like an Italian stiletto knife, right under the ribs.

'Well, lucky me,' she forced out airlessly. 'What a near miss.'

He bent his head just slightly, because he was already worryingly close, and his breath feathered her ear.

'Nowhere near, *cara*,' he said.

Three little words and everything—her stomach, her anger and her somehow connected fizz of arousal—all dropped away with a clang.

He turned around and unlocked the gate, giving it a good shove. He seemed angry all of a sudden. He had no right to be. *She* was the one being pushed around, insulted.

Yet suddenly all she felt was shut out.

The gate creaked and the door broke open onto a brightly lit road outside. He walked through and waited for her on the other side.

Ava came blinking out into the bright southern light. It was hot, but she felt cold, and her attention wasn't on her surroundings. It was on his words.

Feeling a little lost, she found herself blurting out her uncertainties.

'I did not come on to you. I did not bat my eyes and—and lift up my skirt.'

'As you say.'

'I might have been drunk last night, but I'd remember that.'

'*Si*, you were.'

'Were what?'

'Drunk.'

Ava tried to shake off the feeling that she had lost something she'd almost had her hand on for a moment in that garden.

'Oh, and you were *such* a gentleman!'

'Yes, I was.'

He said it with such lethal quiet that she shivered and really didn't want to hear what came next. She watched him walk ahead of her down the winding road. A vista of pine treetops and a glimpse of blue sea lay before them. It was so incredibly lovely, but all Ava wanted to do was grab him and shake him and…and *prove* to him there was something between them.

The realisation brought her up short.

Was that what this was all about? Was he right? Was she here because she *did* want to spend more time with him?

'I did not take advantage of you,' he repeated, 'and yet you harp on about it as if you are disappointed, *cara*. You can't have it both ways. Either you attempted to avail yourself of this reputation of mine you speak of, or you drank so much alcohol last night you no longer cared. I can't say that either of those scenarios reflect well on you, but go ahead and choose and we will abide by that version.'

Ava gaped at him. The sun suddenly felt harsh and unbearable, beating down on the back of her vulnerable neck.

She began to jog a little to keep up with him.

'It wasn't like that at all. You've just twisted everything!'

He shrugged, boredom implicit in the gesture. 'I am no longer interested in any of this, Ava. If you want to justify your own behaviour go and talk it out with a therapist—isn't that what women like you do?'

'Women like me?' she parroted.

'Highly strung, too much time on your hands, with sexual needs that obviously aren't being met.'

Ava absorbed the impact of his opinion of her. It was wrong. It was *so* wrong. He had it all *wrong*.

But somehow in that moment she thought he might be right.

Playboy. Lothario. User of women. Slave to his libido.

Where did she get this from?

He unlocked the doors and shoved them open, waiting for the dust to settle before he moved inside.

Anyone who hitches up her skirt and bats her eyelashes...

Yet he'd heard those words before, hadn't he? And from thinner, far harsher lips.

His father, yelling so hard his face had turned puce. Spittle hitting the wall. Himself, seven years younger—a lifetime ago, it seemed now, shoving his broad young shoulders back and, for the first time in their disastrous relationship, giving back as good as he got. *Better.* He was signing a second contract with the Italian team, he had no intention of doing military service, and as for his social life if he wanted to screw every last woman in Rome he'd give it his best shot.

Was that when the pains had started? Had his unnatural colour been the first sign? Could he have stepped in even then, put his arm around his father, eased him into a chair, fetched the doctor, an ambulance—assistance?

It was never going to go away—the guilt—and damn Ava Lord for bringing it all up again.

He'd left her on the roadside, not trusting himself with her until his temper cooled off. He'd had to get off the mountain, and the usual scenic way—the steps that plunged down the side of a cliff to the road below—was not available to a woman who turned milk-white a hundred feet in the air.

Maybe that was why he'd landed them both on the coast—the gesture of a man who was used to women falling in with his plans, no questions asked. He'd stumbled badly there. But that glimpse of vulnerability in the air had made him want to look after her.

Throwing her off the cliff in a sack would have been the way one of his ancestors would have dealt with her.

He would have to be more creative.

He pulled the tarpaulin cover off the bike, kicked out the stand and pushed it onto the road.

She wasn't like any woman he'd ever known. Something about fighting with her was turning him on, and he was a man who made it a point of honour not to involve himself in disputes with women. He'd seen too many of them growing up, between his parents. They were inevitably messy and emotional, and a man never won.

No, women didn't fight with him… They pouted and sulked and made silly little threats, but in the end they did exactly what they were supposed to do. Looked good and provided a little light entertainment.

Yet in the last two days he'd been angered, provoked, amazed, and he was in the grip of a powerful combination of feelings—primarily sexual. *Si*, he could vouch for the sexual, and it was definitely starting to become painful.

Dressed as she was, spitting insults at him, the antithesis of everything feminine and polished—he still wanted her with a fierce pull that was beyond his previous experience.

That she seemed utterly ignorant of her power over him was the saving grace.

Although he was beginning to think even that was wilful. Crazy woman. He started the bike up. It purred like a kitten. A slow smile curved his mouth. She'd love this. She could hardly sulk on the back of the Ducati.

'*Grazie bene. Molto bene.* This has been most kind of you.'

Having exhausted her schoolgirl Italian, Ava waited and waved to the old man as he made his way back down the path towards a stone foundry.

She stood in the dappled sunshine by a water pump, wondering what Gianluca was doing. Probably at the hotel already, kicking back with some sort of exotic drink and a blonde who, in Ava's imagination, resembled to the letter Donatella… He'd probably sent some lackey looking for her when he'd found her gone, so he didn't have to explain to his precious family how he'd lost her.

Screwing up her face, she mimicked the blonde in her mind. *Oh, Gianluca, you're so wonderful, everything you do is wonderful, let me take off more clothing...*

She ground her teeth together.

Far better that she concentrated on what she could improve for herself. It had been a long day, and it wasn't over by a long shot. She should take this time to regroup, not to fixate on Gianluca Benedetti's sex life and her lack of one.

It was private here, cooler too. Paolo had told her she was welcome to stay as long as she wished, but they would be leaving at five, using an old track direct to the village, and she was welcome to go with them. He'd given her a clay jug to fill with water and she concentrated on filling it.

She had no intention of hanging around. She'd essay that track by herself. But first she wanted to freshen up. She felt hot and sweaty in her clothes, but something about concentrating on the water splashing into the jug was bringing her a measure of peace.

After a quick reconnaissance of the area she determined she was alone and removed her shirt. She splashed cold water from the tap all over her arms and back, chest and belly. It trickled into the waistband of her accursed trousers and she was oh so tempted to rip them off too. But that would have to wait until she was behind a closed door. She determined one thing. When she got back to Sydney she was making a bonfire of them—all twelve pairs—and then she was going on a sexual rampage through the adult male population of Sydney. He'd see who was highly strung and sexually frustrated then!

CHAPTER TEN

GIANLUCA COULDN'T BELIEVE what he was seeing.

She was half stripped and pouring water over herself from a jug. Pouring it over bare, gleaming skin. The clear water, shot with gold at this angle, was gushing out of the pump and Ava had bent over to plunge her arms underneath it, splashing water down her back. She stood up and shook herself completely unselfconsciously.

She jiggled. *Everything* jiggled.

He found himself scanning the area for perverts even as he advanced on her, not entirely sure what his purpose was at this point.

He'd come back for her with the bike, only to spend the last half hour tracking her down. Naturally she'd come back into the garden and wound up at the foundry, but instead of finding a contrite woman he discovered a wood nymph.

She must have heard his tread, but she ignored him and ran more water over the back of her neck, then cupped her hands and brought some into her mouth.

It was too much. He reached down and cut off the flow with an aggressive snap.

'Hey!' she coughed.

He shoved her shirt at her. 'Cover yourself up.'

She turned around and his gaze instantly dropped to her breasts, to the gleaming, glistening rivulets of water running down those slopes in a race to see which was going to soak the white cotton bra first.

He recognised that she was saying something but it got lost in the roar of testosterone currently running at full throttle through him—the kind of overload that made a man say, do, be anything required to stay perfectly still, beholding something designed to turn him into a blithering idiot.

His gaze dropped a little further to the revelation of how her ribs narrowed to a beautifully indented waist, and below her hips flared out almost outrageously. The ugly trousers had lost their top button and hung from the widest point of her hips, revealing her navel and a masterpiece of a soft female belly. Like most men, he really wasn't enamoured of a flat female stomach, and his fingers flexed as he resisted the temptation to touch her there, to stroke her, to test the softness, before his hand moved lower...

He distinctly heard her say, 'Get a grip, Benedetti.'

His attention bounced back to her breasts. The bra was definitely opaque now. Strawberry pink nipples were visible.

Astounded by his lack of self-control, he snarled at her, 'Put the shirt on—*Dio*!'

When she just stood there, blinking like a rabbit in a gun's sights, he took hold of one of her hands and began pushing it through an armhole.

She jerked away from him and hurriedly pulled the shirt over her shoulders, turning her back on him.

He took a couple of steps back, struck by the way he was behaving. Like a madman.

So what if she was standing around in her underwear? He'd had girlfriends in the past who didn't seem to possess a bikini top, who paraded around poolside, and frankly he couldn't have cared less.

Why had he complicated something so utterly simple with this farce? He should never have brought her here. He should have withstood his desire to have her to himself and kept to his plan to take her to Ragusa. Instead he now had her halfway up a mountain with very limited options for getting her down. He should be focussing on those logistics, not on this overwhelming need to corral her. He would explain to her about traditional attitudes and the need to respect them. She would keep herself buttoned up. She would behave, in truth, like the twenty-year-old Sicilian virgin his mother would prefer him to marry. Only then could he relax.

He watched Ava fighting her way into her shirt, muttering something about him being a prude, all the while trying to cover herself up. Her head was bent and he could see the soft kiss curls made by her hair at the base of her neck, at odds with her unforgiving clothes.

Tenderness unexpectedly backhanded him.

When Ava had heard him coming her heart leapt because he'd actually come looking for her. But her first instinct—to be modest, to cover herself up—she had thrown aside.

After all, stab-your-heart-out-blondes didn't have a problem with advertising their wares.

Oh, she'd known she was playing with fire, but deep down an entirely feminine part of her psyche had wanted a little payback.

Sexually frustrated, was she? Well, two could play at that game.

But he'd looked at her as if he was made of stone.

She'd thought her breasts looked pretty good in this bra. Not perky—you couldn't be her size and shoot for the moon… although given this man had had close personal contact with some spectacularly beautiful women he was probably used to the stay-up-on-their-own-thanks-to-a-surgeon variety.

Ava shut down on that line of thought. It didn't help.

'The people here are conservative,' he imparted roughly. 'This isn't your Bondi Beach, with its topless women, and nor is it Positano. This is part of a small mountain village. Show some respect.'

Still feeling beleaguered by all those gorgeous women with more noteworthy breasts he had access to—no doubt he didn't yell at *them* and do his best to cover them up—Ava lost her temper.

'Respect?' she muttered, fumbling with the buttons. 'Why don't you start showing *me* some respect? This whole mess is all your fault to begin with. You're the one who wanted to take the scenic tour of Italy…'

She turned around, only to find he was standing right behind her. She looked up and blinked. He had an odd, entirely too satisfied look on his face.

She gave a soft gasp as he picked her up and tossed her potato-sack fashion over his shoulder.

'Put me down!' she shrieked. But apparently one hundred and fifty pounds of wriggling woman didn't deter a man who had been pushed to his limit, and Ava was getting the distinct impression this might be the case.

As he waded through the undergrowth she stopped struggling and sagged a little against him. Gianluca only put her down when they reached the road.

She spotted the red Ducati immediately.

'What's this?'

'Transport down the mountain.'

As he spoke he straddled the bike.

Ava's feet had frozen. She was *not* strapping herself to his back on that thing.

'Sorry, Benedetti. Been there, done that…'

'Get on the bike, Ava.'

Something about the tone of his voice, the fact he was not quite looking at her, and the way she was feeling—tired, confused, and a little overwhelmed at seeing the bike—had her doing as he asked.

He fired up the four-stroke engine. It purred and crackled with energy. She approached and slid carefully onto the seat. There wasn't much room. Her pelvis was smack up against his hard rear, her inner thighs pressing against his lean, muscled hips. She held herself as stiffly as she could, but he was big and warm and solid, and as they took off her hands groped instinctively for his waist. She tightened them over slabs of hard muscle and heat and swore she felt them move.

Her thighs melted as if on cue. This was *not* good.

The bike leapt as they hit the road. He took the corners on the narrow ribbon of mountain road at speed. Without helmets there was some risk involved. But something else was riding him. She could feel the tension in his big body. Which was just fine by her, because none of this was her idea of fun either. Except for the part about her entire body buzzing and tingling like an electrical storm. But she put that down to proximity and friction.

'Next time remind me to take a bus,' she commented as he braked and they pulled over to allow a small car to pass on the single road ribboning down the mountain.

'*Si?* You would last five minutes, *cara*. The minute you opened that fine mouth of yours the driver would dump you on the roadside.'

She relaxed slightly. This was good. This she could do.

'Careful, Benedetti, or I'll jump off—and how are you going to explain *that* to your mother and Alessia?'

'Believe me, *bella*, once they meet you nobody will question me for dumping you.'

He gunned the engine and they took off again.

Ava guessed she deserved that one. If she was going to dish them out, she had to take them. But she knew well enough that neither woman liked her particularly, and the reminder recalled her to the reality of her situation. She'd almost forgotten in the excitement what this was all about, and her heart started to thump to an irregular, painful beat she recognised.

'Hold on,' he instructed, and he angled them off the road where they hit an unsealed track. Within minutes it became increasingly rocky.

Bouncing behind him, she shouted, 'This wasn't your best idea!'

'It's a damn sight safer than the road,' he responded grimly, 'and the benefit is, you get to live.'

'With bruises on my posterior!'

'Keep looking at the upside, *cara*.'

They hit a rut and her bottom came down hard on the seat. She moaned.

'You did that on purpose!'

'Sometimes fate takes a hand.'

This wasn't fun any more. She was tired of all the fighting, mostly engineered by herself, to keep him at arm's length. But he seemed to be taking some enjoyment in shaking her up. She fell quiet, concentrating on not coming down too hard on the seat.

To her surprise he was braking gently, gradually bringing the bike to a halt. His movements were careful, deliberate. The brake, the ignition, the footrest. The dreadful sudden silence.

Ava looked around at the craggy rocks rising up above them and for some reason she panicked.

'What now?' she asked nervously. 'You get off, push the bike into the ravine and I'm never heard of again?'

He shifted around and she jerked back, unable to unhook her legs. She was stuck. On a bike, in the back of beyond, with a man who seemed to be all brawn and muscle. And she'd been poking him with a big sharp stick. All day.

His golden eyes moved over her with unsettling directness, and under his scrutiny she could feel her cheeks starting to burn.

'We need to get this out of our systems,' he asserted roughly.

Ava could have put her hand over her heart in that moment and sworn it was the last thing she'd expected him to say.

'S-sorry?'

'What is the Australian saying? We need to screw like rabbits until the novelty's worn off.'

Ava gaped. 'We *what*?'

'Is the vernacular wrong?'

She was about to tell him exactly how wrong he was, even as her pulse sped up, when she caught the glint in his golden eyes from beneath those sinfully thick black lashes and everything painful and wrong about her life tumbled away.

He wasn't laughing at her, she realised. He was including her in the joke. And with that a very important piece of that long-ago jigsaw moved into place. She remembered—*this was how he'd made her feel*. As if she wasn't on the outside looking in any more. As if it were all about him and her, their own exclusive little club.

'Yes, the vernacular is wrong,' she said a little faintly.

He smiled at her and she felt her heart lift, as if it were attached to strings connected to his wide, sensual mouth.

Her own mouth twitched. She was *not* going to laugh.

'And I can assure you that won't be happening,' she followed up quickly. But as much as she tried to sound prim and decisive it all collapsed as everything tense and painful inside her unravelled.

He reached over and did something so unexpected she stopped breathing. He cradled her cheek with his hand, forcing her to look at him, following the curve of her cheekbone gently with the pad of his thumb.

'So we are agreed?'

She wanted to push his hand away, bristle like a cat under a pail of water, but this sudden gentleness on his part brought her ridiculously ready emotions to the surface. She blinked rapidly.

'You remind me of those little porcupines, rolling into a ball of bristles to protect yourself, but underneath you have this soft, velvety little belly.'

'Porcupines are rodents,' she retorted, wondering if that reference to her belly was because, unlike the women he dated, *she* had one. 'Trust you to compare me to a pest.'

Then she realised she'd just scrambled to protect herself—exactly as he'd said.

'What is it you're running from? What is it that threatens you, Ava?' His voice was quiet and he continued to stroke her.

Her heart was fluttering wildly. She could feel herself wanting to lean against him, of all things wanting to confide in him, tell him how confused she was feeling, being back here in Italy with him, wondering if she had made a terrible mistake seven years ago and not wanting to make a worse one now.

She looked into his eyes and he smiled. 'You find me attractive, *si*? It is nothing to be ashamed of.'

Saved by his ego! She knocked his hand away. Just as all sorts of longings had risen to the surface they were swamped by his incredible arrogance. 'Oh, yes, *all* women must find you utterly irresistible. It just must gall you to know I'm immune.'

'Immune?' His fingers, so gentle on her cheek, drummed lightly on the frame of the bike. 'How much easier this would be if you were. I wouldn't have to put up with your constant attention-seeking.'

'Attention-*what*? I'm doing nothing of the sort.' She looked away, because if she was honest it was a whopper of a lie. She had been enjoying having his whole attention all day. 'It's just your colossal ego,' she muttered.

'I seem to remember you admired my ego seven years ago, *cara*.'

Ava swung around. 'I don't want to talk about that!'

'Yes, you do,' he growled. 'It's all you want to talk about.'

Caught off guard by the truth, she lashed out. 'I was stupid. You took advantage of me!'

'You were the older woman,' he inserted with that incredible cool.

Ava shot him an incredulous look. 'I can't believe you're throwing my age at me!'

He made an impatient gesture of disbelief with one hand and with another movement slid his hand into the backpack strapped behind the bike. He uncapped a bottle and thrust it at her.

'What's that for?'

'To cool you down. I don't have a bucket of water to hand.'

'I'm not the one talking about rabbits,' she grumbled, irritated because she was breathless all of a sudden. Even fighting with him turned her on. This was most unlike her! She took a swallow and handed it back to him.

He didn't wipe the rim, just took a swig. Ava watched the muscles working in his throat and tried not to stare.

It was so unfair. Everything about him made her want to jump him.

She literally *felt* him smile as he recapped the bottle.

'I would never have slept with you if I'd been in the right frame of mind that night,' she muttered, more to herself than to him.

He stilled, and the easy amusement was suddenly long gone. *'Cosa?'*

She hadn't meant it, but she discovered she couldn't back down. If she did he would see too much—her fear of intimacy—and he'd put two and two together. She feared that exposure more than his anger.

'You heard me.' She avoided his eyes. 'I was upset and not thinking straight and you were in like a shot.'

'I think you should get your facts straight, Signorina Lord,' he drawled, those golden eyes watchful, 'before you start making accusations.'

Ava swallowed hard, staring past him, chin up. She *so* didn't want to have this conversation here and now. It was too intimate, there was nowhere to run to, and he was right beside her—seeing too much, holding the power to slice and dice her fragile ego.

'You threw yourself at me,' he observed, as if he were commenting on the weather.

Ava flinched.

'You did it last night, and you did it seven years ago,' he continued remorselessly. 'It seems to be your modus operandi, *tesoro*. I'm guessing I shouldn't feel flattered.'

As she absorbed the impact of his opinion of her the motorbike's engine roared into life again and Ava gripped the hard column of his waist.

He didn't say anything else all the way down the mountain—because, really, what more was there to say?

CHAPTER ELEVEN

THE HOTEL, LIKE EVERYTHING about Gianluca Benedetti, was not what she'd expected. It was subtle and charming and took advantage of the best water views in Positano.

As he crossed the foyer, shirt half unbuttoned, sleeves shoved up to the elbows, hand-tooled shoes dusty and scuffed, Gianluca still managed to look like an advertisement for a high-end men's fragrance—one of those where a guy came out of water or walked down a beach or gazed knowingly over the naked body of a lithe, bronzed woman.

Ava was all too aware she looked like a woman who had been dragged backwards through the underbrush.

A posse of beautiful leggy girls on their way out fluttered and smiled and broke into a flurry of giggles as Gianluca held the door for them.

Completely unnecessary, as far as Ava could see. They had arms and hands, didn't they?

One of the women stopped to speak to him. Did he *have* to linger?

Flirt.

Her heart started to pound, and not in a good way. Well, that was fine. She could look after herself.

She folded her arms and looked around. She spotted the welcome desk and headed over.

She was just handing over her passport when a deep voice intruded, 'She has a room, Pietro.'

Ava ignored him.

'As I was saying, I would like a single.'

But the desk clerk was looking over her shoulder. Frustrated, Ava rounded on Gianluca. 'Could you butt out?'

He merely looked at her, with stone-cold disapproval, and Ava's bravado-meter dipped.

Because she was behaving this way for the most obvious reason. She was jealous.

'Notice me!' was what she wanted to say. But what would he notice? A tired, grubby, irritable woman who had done nothing but snipe at him all day.

'I'm sorry,' she said, sounding stiff and all wrong yet again. 'That was rude of me—'

'It's been a long day already, Ava, and I have business to attend to,' he interrupted. 'I'll have a car made ready for you in the morning to take you on to Rome, or Ragusa. Whichever you prefer.'

What she preferred was to put her head on his shoulder and apologise for every horrible thing she'd said today, to have him cradle her face with his hands again as he had on the bike, and not to look at other women.

That was never going to happen now, and she was feeling too tired and sorry for herself to get mad about it.

In the lift he took out his phone, which was as good a message as any from where she stood. Enclosed in a small space with him, she couldn't help inhaling the scent of him. He smelled so good, even after all the tramping around, the bumping through underbrush on that motorcycle. He smelled of hot male skin and grass and salt and a little bit of petrol fumes from the bike.

It was a heady combination on him, but probably not so entrancing on her, and she held herself even more stiffly, folding her arms, wishing she could just vanish into merciful invisibility.

A furtive glance at their reflection in the mirrored walls only reinforced the contrast, and Ava realised in a rush of self-actualisation that he was right. These clothes did her no favours.

When had she started dressing this way? When had not wanting to draw attention to herself become a kind of self-obliteration? Bernard had said a woman in her position, with her figure, needed to be careful. So she *was* careful. High-necked blouses. No skirts. Nothing that would draw attention to her femininity.

No wonder it was no skin off Gianluca's nose if she was in Ragusa or Rome or wherever.

On their floor, he keyed open a door and stepped back to allow her inside.

She had expected something like the luxury sports car he drove—state-of-the-art, a little bit flashy, lots of grunt. A Gianluca Benedetti signature.

Instead he'd booked her into a boutique hotel which seemed to be something out of a Grimm's fairy tale, with wood inlay on the walls, cool patterned parquet underfoot and a mix of charming antique and quirky contemporary furniture. She took in the arched and vaulted doorways and windows, which would make the occupants feel they were inside something not of this era and quite wonderful. Unexpectedly she felt close to tears.

'This is my room?' she asked in wonder, turning around with an open look on her face. She remembered he had said something about it belonging to a friend. She wondered if she could use it as a conversation-opener, to show him she could be as charming, approachable, *friendly* as those silly girls downstairs.

She cleared her throat and what came out was, 'I really must insist on paying—'

The door shut in her face with a neat click.

For a moment Ava didn't move.

He had never actually been rude to her before, and a part of her brain said it was clearly another message. He had held that door wide for those girls. He had smiled and lingered like

Prince Charming. Then turned around and slammed a door in her face.

Yes, it was difficult to ignore that door now several inches from her face.

She wasn't sure how she got to the bathroom. She wasn't really aware she was taking off her clothes until the buttons felt fiddly under her fingers. When they wouldn't shift fast enough she began ripping her shirt off. It wasn't as if she had to worry about ruining it—she had a thousand more lined up in her closet at home…

She extended her trousers scarcely more care, because really they didn't deserve it.

Standing in her underwear, she gave her reflection in the mirror a good look. Although of simple white cotton, the set cost more than some people made in a week of work.

There was no use denying that after Gianluca had swept in to her hotel room this morning she'd set aside her usual granny undies to shimmy her way into these.

What a fraud she was.

She hit the shower cubicle, snapping on the jets. The water pounded down on her head as she lathered herself up with the luxury vanilla and clove-scented soap—as far from her own scentless plain bar of soap in her toiletries bag as could be. She washed her dust-laden hair with the complementary products and waited for the warm water to work its magic on her tense muscles.

Instead she had to do battle against the memory of hard hips and thighs between her legs, the feel of a long, broad and muscular back, the clench of rock-hard abdominal muscles under her hands.

The ache low in her pelvis taunted her.

What are you going to do about it, Ava? whispered a hateful voice. *He thinks you're uptight and frustrated and in need of a shrink.*

She hung her head and let the water cascade down.

It was no use.

He was a man who dated models and actresses and hosted private parties at ritzy bars where girls wearing almost nothing draped themselves over him… She was a woman who made lists in her head during sex, when she wasn't sucking in her tummy and trying to hide her bottom.

It would never work.

Yet he was also a man who flew helicopters in war zones, and had cared enough to try and calm her fears of the helicopter. She lifted her head. And when it had come to getting her out of a bind today he'd come through.

She tried to imagine Bernard with her on the hillside. She would have been responsible for getting them both down.

Ava snapped off the flow of water and stepped out before she drowned herself. She was feeling truly wretched by the time she'd towel-dried her hair, rubbed lotion into her skin and gone in search of fresh clothes.

She couldn't quite bring herself to pull on another pair of long trousers, and it wasn't as if she was going anywhere, so she stepped into the boy-leg shorts she slept in and a blue stretchy cotton camisole before brushing out her hair.

She'd order room service and phone the office, check in with her assistant, PJ.

Except it was the wee hours of the morning in Australia.

Which meant, robbed of her go-to, she would have to find something else to keep her mind occupied.

The rest of the afternoon stretched out before her…and the rest of her fearful, boxed-up life which she had come to Italy to change.

She plopped down on the bed and looked around unhappily. She'd come to the conclusion she'd stuffed this up. But was she woman enough to fix it?

Gianluca only half listened to the earnest conversation of his lawyer as he sat at a table with his legals and a Russian oligarch.

Most women would be *grateful* to be dropped onto the

Italian Riviera for a couple days of R & R. In point of fact he could think of several just off the cuff who would brawl with one another to have the chance of spending a couple of days in his company in these surroundings... He was known for being generous. He didn't begrudge a woman a little shopping, a little pampering—it always made them far more relaxed and amenable when it came to the point for which they were both here.

Si, there were many women who would appreciate this gesture.

Clearly Ava wasn't one of them.

She had a sharp tongue, that female, and no sense at all of her role as a woman—to smooth the awkward moment, to expect his assistance.

Instead she pushed him to treat her as he would a man—but what she didn't understand was that if a man had behaved as she had today he'd be out cold on that hillside right now, not sitting nice and tight in a luxury hotel.

Basta. He'd spent too much valuable time thinking about this. He'd done his duty by her. He could live with the papers' stories about his supposed latest squeeze—he was used to it, after all. As far as he was concerned there was no need for them to see one another again.

Besides, there was a cure for this. This was Positano. There were beautiful, available women everywhere. Fiery, opinionated Italian women, who knew how to handle a man, knew when to challenge and when to lay down their weapons and offer up some much appreciated docility.

He observed one or two of these paragons as he sipped his vodka.

The Russian, who had flown in for this one-hour face-to-face and would be flying out afterwards to join his mistress on his super-yacht at St Tropez, followed suit.

The lawyers continued to buzz.

When the business of the day was set aside the Russian leaned casually back in his chair and said in his soft, thickly accented Italian, 'Fly out with me this evening, Gianluca. We can look at the plans over dinner.'

The plans. Drinks and dinner. A bevy of the beautiful girls who travelled the world with one of Europe's richest men. The oligarch was infamous for his parties. But Gianluca's thoughts flickered not to tanned skin and lithe, flexible female bodies, but to Australia's answer to Gina Lollobrigida, wagging her finger at him and lecturing him about Seventies-era James Bond. He wondered what kind of response the Russian would get from her.

Which was when he laughed for the first time since she'd accused him of being a playboy. Which was when he knew he wouldn't be going anywhere. What he wanted was right here in Positano.

CHAPTER TWELVE

AVA SAT UP GROGGILY. She was in the middle of the bed and a quilt she couldn't remember drawing over herself was crumpled under her hand.

She hadn't meant to fall asleep. She remembered lying down and feeling so lousy it had almost hurt to take her next breath. She rubbed her eyes listlessly. Clearly she'd underestimated the toll the day had taken on her.

The quality of light drifting through the windows was different—softer. Some time must have passed. Ava froze. There was a sports coat draped over one of the high-backed chairs, and keys and a phone on the table. Even as she kicked her legs free of the quilt she listened. Running water. It was the shower.

Ava propelled herself off the bed, her hands going to her hair, madly smoothing it down.

He was in her shower—*their* shower. Were they sharing a room? He hadn't said anything about sharing a room. Typical! It was a huge presumption on his behalf. Especially when he knew her feelings on the subject...

Ava caught herself mid-tirade.

Her feelings had changed.

Somehow, at some point coming down that mountain, her feelings had changed.

And she was doing it again. Working herself up to avoid facing her fears.

She subsided back onto the bed.

He'd come back to her.

She bit her lip and smiled the smallest smile.

Think, Ava, think. Remember what he said about you being sexually frustrated and highly strung? You could show him. You could make him eat those words.

There was only one teeny, tiny problem—and, given he was a sex god, he might not even notice.

She wasn't very good at it.

Sex.

But maybe there was an opportunity here for her...

He had all the skill.

She could take advantage of that.

She was here in this beautiful spot, with one of the sexiest men in the world. She remembered *very* successful sex the last time. Was there ever going to be a more perfect opportunity than this?

Gianluca Benedetti wasn't a man who did deep and meaningful. Knowing that going in, she wouldn't attach herself. It would be sex. If she could just relax and follow the dictates of her body, not her conscience...nor her heart...she would be fine.

Just fine.

She eyed the bathroom door. Perhaps if she just *checked*.

Swallowing hard, she approached the door, carefully laid her ear against the woodwork and listened. Definitely water... and another sound—was he singing?

Somehow the idea that he was singing lifted her spirits. He couldn't be very angry with her if he could hold a tune. Maybe she could just duck her head in and say— What, Ava? *I'm sorry for being defensive. I just hadn't worked out what I wanted, and now I have. I want you. I want you so much I think I might die of it.*

The worst he could do was say no.

He would probably say no.

Would he say no?

The shower partition would be fogged. She wouldn't even

look. And if, say, she glimpsed the shadow of his body behind the opaque glass she'd hardly be breaking any great taboos. Everyone knew men were a lot less modest about these things than women.

Any further reasoning dissolved as she was hit by steam, a partition that wasn't opaque at all, and six feet six inches of naked male, with spread shoulders, a long, broad back and taut, streamlined buttocks above long, powerful legs.

Gianluca stood with his face in the water stream, drenching his hair to black, and he *was* singing. His voice was a deep, rich baritone, and of course the Italian made everything so much more resonant.

He was just about the sexiest thing Ava had ever seen.

If she backed out now he'd never know she'd been there, but she simply couldn't take her eyes off him.

She told herself she was thirty-one years old. She'd seen plenty of men naked in showers... All right, *two*. Two perfectly nice, athletic, healthy men of around six feet—average men.

He turned around, eyes closed, throwing back his head under the spray, drawing one arm up to soap the back of his neck. The breath stuck in Ava's throat as her eyes dropped to the prize.

Gianluca Benedetti wasn't average.

He opened his eyes and hot molten gold stared back at her through black lashes stuck together with droplets of water. His gaze dropped to her unfettered breasts and Ava just knew her nipples were doing all sorts of interesting things as her body went into meltdown.

She drank in his olive skin, the dark shadow of chest hair arrowing down to the hard, compact ridges of his abdomen, and his beautiful penis, swelling, darkening with arousal before her eyes.

How can he find me attractive in my boy-leg shorts when I don't have stick-thin legs?

It was one of those puzzles, like the mystery of the *Mary Celeste*, destined to go unsolved. But there was no doubt he was looking her over with an expression that would have put any woman's body issues to rest.

He said something basic in Italian and Ava gave a little gasp as naked, dripping, pumping testosterone, he picked her up as if she was a featherweight and dragged her into the shower, making a cushion of his arm for her as he flattened her against the tiles and kissed her. Just like that. His tongue was in her mouth, his stubble was rubbing against her skin, and her lips felt caressed and devoured all at the same time. She hadn't known kissing could be like this.

He dwarfed her with the size of his shoulders. They were a wall she couldn't climb. But she wound her arms up around his neck anyway.

Up, up, up... He was the only man she'd ever kissed she'd had to reach up to. It was a completely different experience.

Yes, that was it—his height, and his build...the big, hard, masculine body she was sliding against which made him impossible for her to resist. It was the water that made everything far too slippery. She couldn't help the circular motion of her hips against him, wordlessly encouraging the pulsing industrial-strength push of his erection against her rounded belly.

His hands were around her waist, under her sopping camisole, peeling it up. *'Il seno bello,'* he growled, and Ava was suddenly hyper-aware of the heaviness of her breasts as her erogenous zones leapt into action.

One big hand cupped the underside of her left breast as he bent and sucked her nipple into his mouth through the wet cotton, rubbing it with his teeth until she was positively shaking. He did the same with the other, his hands pushing down her shorts, finding the bare curve of her behind and squeezing with a gratified groan of appreciation.

The water felt warm as it sprayed over her, his mouth was hot and slick wherever it strayed, and all she could do was hang on to him, stroking the hard, hot expanse of his shoulders and back, his chest, wishing she was better at this. It was as if she'd played all her life at local level and had then been recruited into the big league. She wove her fingers through his hair and brought his head up to hers again, kissed him as passionately and wantonly as she felt.

'Are you protected?' he asked her in Italian, his voice almost guttural.

Ava nodded vigorously, even as she kept kissing him.

'*Preservativo,*' he told her, his mouth moving away from hers, hot against her throat. 'I've got condoms. I'll use one if you'd prefer.'

She almost told him no, and then with a sort of terrible clarity she remembered. He was playboy of the western world. God knew how many other women he'd slept with just this month, let alone this year. It had been seven years since she'd last been in his arms. She'd been with Patrick very briefly—and he had always used condoms—and then Bernard, her plodding, safe relationship. Gianluca had probably worked his way through the adult female population of Italy...

Something pinched inside her chest and Ava felt her pulse begin to speed up—and not in a good way.

Don't think about all that, the new, reckless Ava urged. *Just go for it. Have your little frolic in the shower, enjoy what he has to offer, and move on with your life. Isn't that what this is all about? Putting the past behind you, making things over in a better way...?*

She pushed her hands against his chest. 'I want you to wear a condom,' she told him, making a space between them.

'*Si,*' he assured her, and then his tongue was in her mouth again.

She shoved at him. 'No—go and do it now.'

He didn't answer. He merely shut off the water flow, picked her up and carried her wet and dripping out into the bedroom.

He dumped her on the bed and dived for his toiletries bag. Ava sat up, pulling down her camisole. Her stomach only began to plummet when he tipped the bag onto the floor.

'You don't have condoms?'

Gianluca hissed out a breath between his teeth and met her

accusatory gaze. He was so beautiful, aroused and predatory—everything she had fantasised about for so long…

It made her furious!

'I cannot *believe* you of all people don't have condoms!'

He was looking at her strangely. 'Calm down, *cara*. I will make a phone call.'

Ava's jaw dropped slightly. 'Room service provides prophylactics?'

'Why not?'

Aching in places she hadn't ached for a very long time, Ava found herself scrambling to her knees.

'Maybe this isn't a good idea.'

Gianluca stilled. 'What has changed?'

Ava crossed her arms over her breasts. She might as well be topless in the wet fabric, and suddenly everything didn't seem so spur-of-the-moment any more. She felt exposed and wanted to hide away.

He looked incredible. He made her knees wobble, her heart shake, rattle and roll in her chest. She shook her head, knowing she had to be strong and resist.

She felt like bursting into tears.

What was *wrong* with her?

Without a word Gianluca strode to the wardrobe, yanked out a pair of jeans and shoved his legs into them, easing them over what ailed him. Then he grabbed a shirt, punching his arms through the sleeves.

'Wh-what are you doing?'

'Wait there.'

Ava scrambled off the bed, but in a single step, with an outstretched arm, he had her up against him—masculine, potent, dangerous. She trembled, but didn't resist as he clasped her chin and planted a fierce kiss on her amazed mouth.

'Wait,' he said.

'I'm not—' she began, but he was gone.

She heard the main door slam.

She slumped on the bed for a full minute, just thinking

about consequences, and what might happen tomorrow, and how if she didn't have him inside her a part of her might shrivel up and die. But if she did she would have to give something else up. The memory of that shining night when she'd shared her soul with him. And that had meant something.

Because she was going to stuff this up.

Sex wasn't something she was any good at. Patrick and Bernard had found her disappointing; it could only be catastrophic with a sex god like Gianluca. All her earlier feelings of being sexy and wanting something more had shrivelled down to a pile of self-doubt.

She briefly considered making a run for it, packing up her things and vanishing before he returned. But she'd been a coward once before, and how was she going to face him in Ragusa on Sunday if she ran now? No, she had started this, and she always saw things through. When he realised she was no good all this would just *stop*.

Wiping at her damp eyes, she stripped off her wet things and wrapped herself in her big white robe. She had barely covered up when the door banged open. Gianluca was framed in it, looking like every fantasy any red-blooded woman could have, and all the arguments she had assembled collapsed as he threw several boxes onto the bed.

'Where did you get those from?' Her tongue suddenly felt too big for her mouth.

'Farmacia,' he said.

'You went into a chemist's?'

'Si.' A slight smile edged his mouth. 'Why aren't you naked?'

She ignored that, even though her knees felt wobbly. 'Are you planning on sleeping with a lot of women while you're here?'

'I think my time will be taken up with you, *bella,'* he said, advancing on her.

'But four boxes?' She backed up and her bottom hit the wall. How had she ended up all the way over here?

'I was in a hurry,' he said, shrugging it off.

Ava's fears, arguments and nonsensical reasoning dried up.

He hadn't planned this. He hadn't planned any of it! Wouldn't a man with seduction on his mind have armed himself with the necessaries? Didn't a guy like him come with a kit they handed out at Playboys Incorporated? All of her preconceptions were breaking down because this didn't feel standard or routine. He wasn't acting as if this meant nothing.

He'd gone out and found a chemist—*like an ordinary person.*

Ava saw the fierce urgency in his expression, the way he was watching her—like a lion eying a gazelle he was preparing to take down. It reminded her there was nothing ordinary about Gianluca Benedetti, and although they had been together before he was older now, a great deal had changed, and she had spent the last seven years learning how disappointing she was in bed.

Yet he'd brought back condoms. She felt as if he'd gone out and slain dragons for her.

'What about your meetings?' she asked on a deep swallow.

'What meetings?'

He leaned over her, one arm caging her in as he pressed his hand to the wall above her shoulder, the other deftly dealing with the knotted belt around her waist.

His fingers brushed against her bare belly as the robe fell open, circling her navel. Every sensible thought in her head flew out, probably never to be heard from again.

He drew his fingertips up through the valley between her breasts all the way to brush over her clavicle, then he gently nudged the robe over the curve of her shoulder until it fell a little way down her back, revealing her shoulder and most of one breast.

His eyes grew intent under that heavy fringe of lashes as he traced the edge of the robe on its descent to the outer rim of her nipple.

'Are you sensitive here?'

Ava trembled as he rubbed softly over the puffy pink of her areola. 'Y-yes.'

Why was he asking these questions? Why didn't he just get on with it?

She watched him deftly nudge the cloth west and circle her nipple with his thumb. She gave a little start. She wanted him to use his teeth, like he had in the shower, suck on them hard, make the muscles of her inner thighs clench. She needed him to overwhelm her before she lost her nerve.

She didn't have his confidence. She wasn't very good in bed.

Yet his gentleness was what she wanted too. She hadn't expected it, and she found she wanted it like her next breath.

God help her, it didn't feel like seduction.

He pushed the robe off her other shoulder and it fell heavily to the floor. Ava hoped the dusky light would be kind to her. She was aware of him lightly fondling her breasts as he simply looked at her, as if memorising the fullness of their shape above the narrow span of her waist, the gentle curve of her belly below and the more dramatic rounding of her hips, the tiny dark brown curls guarding her secrets between the solidity of her thighs. Ava knew all of these things about herself. She also knew it was hard for her to be naked with someone and arousal was not an easy thing for her. Yet here she was, humming all over, with energy moving through her body like light, warming her, setting her aglow.

She forced herself to meet his gaze head-on and...

'You are *perfetto*.' His hands smoothed over her breasts, glided down her ribs to spread over the flare of her hips, and he brought her in so close she could feel the tremble in his body.

Okay. This was nice. He was looking at her as if she was a goddess and that just made her feel...

Good. It made her feel good. Strong. Female.

Except shouldn't she be touching him too? She didn't want to be accused of being cold.

Bernard had always complained about her lack of participation, but she would always get lost in her head, start making lists for the next day, and really it had begun and finished too fast for her to warm up.

She wouldn't mind going a little faster right now, because she was feeling extremely warm at this point, no lists in her head. She rested her palms on his chest, her fingers tackling the few buttons he'd managed to do up, touching his chest lightly at first and then with more confidence. He felt so hard—springy flesh over steely muscle. She wasn't used to muscle. She wasn't used to feeling smaller, daintier, *feminine*.

He laid her down on the bed and, holding her hands on the mattress, began to kiss her. Long, slow, mind-blowing kisses, seducing her beyond reason with only his mouth, for the moment denying her his body.

She was aware of him pulling off the shirt, could feel his chest hair abrading her breasts, and she gave an involuntary gasp as his thumb ran over the seam of her sex, parting the folds, dipping inside. She stopped thinking.

Oh, God, everything about her was conspiring to make this easy for him. She gripped him around the neck. She didn't want it to be easy. He didn't deserve easy—not after what he'd done to her.

She felt him kiss the curve of her neck, murmur endearments in Italian, felt his big hands splay over her breasts, tugging at her nipples as he lifted his head to kiss her. The feel of his mouth was so compelling on hers—the slide of his tongue, hers joining his, in an echo of the feel of his fingers against her intimate flesh. He made a low, thrilling growl when she found the bare skin of his chest and tangled her fingers in his hair, dragged circles around his flat male nipples, pressed her mouth there and licked him.

He tasted like salt and male skin and Gianluca. The reason she knew the taste of him flew out of her head, but she did, and it made her crazy with want for him. She slid her hand down to unzip him, but he was doing it himself, shucking his jeans and moving over her with all the predatory grace of a man who knew what he wanted and how to get it.

Ava flexed her hand over the rigid length of him and watched as his beautiful features grew taut and pronounced. She circled the head with her thumb, wondering if she should be worried or happy about his size.

She needed to tell him she wasn't always able to let go, that she might disappoint him. Tears built up in the back of her eyes and she blinked rapidly to stop them from falling. She didn't want this to be a failure. She didn't want to wreck it like she wrecked everything else.

Even as her anxieties drove through her thoughts like an express train her thighs fell open naturally to cradle him. But he wasn't in a hurry. He smoothed her hair off her shoulder, fingered it as if the silky texture fascinated him, and then laid the gentlest kiss on the top of one breast, moving agonisingly slowly to her nipple, to the curve of her hip, her belly...

'If you could just—' she began.

He lifted his mouth momentarily. 'If I could what, *dolcezza*?' he asked, and rimmed her belly button with his tongue.

Ava's stomach convulsed and she gripped the sheets. 'It takes me a while,' she asserted breathlessly, even as it occurred to her that it wasn't taking her very long at all. She was throbbing like a heartbeat between her thighs. 'There are certain things you need to do—ways I need to be touched—*oh*.'

He slid a finger inside her, and then another, and she closed her eyes, lost for a moment in the sensations.

He was speaking to her in Italian again as she shuddered under him.

'Is that good?'

She recognised that bit of English amidst the Italian. 'Good—yes. Oh, yes,' Ava whimpered, and bit her lip as she tried not to cry out. More sensation streaked through her. But his other hand was stroking her face. He was dragging his thumb over her mouth until she was sucking on it, biting down on him as her lower body arched off the mattress.

'Mia ragazza bella,' he told her in a hushed rough voice. *'Lasciarsi andare.'*

'Luca,' she sobbed, and the moment before she cascaded into a million pieces of pleasure she had the satisfaction of seeing his watchful expression turn wild.

He was still watching her with fierce, glittering eyes as he positioned himself, powerfully male above her, and Ava could see the telltale tension in his body as he held himself back. She lifted her body in response, reaching up to push her fingers through his hair.

As he filled her his careful restraint was almost as erotic as the sensation of her tender tissues expanding to encompass him. He watched her the whole time.

'Luca...' she breathed as he sank deep.

'Good, my sweet Ava?'

Her emotions did a figure-eight in her chest, tying her up in knots.

He pushed and their hips locked.

He said something in Italian, in such a way that she knew this was as good for him as it was for her. Perhaps better. His body tremored with the strain of holding back and she smoothed her palms over his hair-roughened chest, wanting the intimacy of this to be preserved in her memory.

For a moment everything seemed to slow down. *It's not your first time.* A faint voice rippled through her senses. *Your body remembers him. You remember him...*

'Now,' she breathed. 'Oh, Luca, now.'

Her hips lifted of their own accord as he began to move deeper. His eyes didn't leave hers and he wasn't asking her if it was good this time. He was driving her to where they both wanted to be and she found she didn't have to think about his rhythm. Her body took it up like a drumbeat.

Oh, God. I feel like I was born to do this with this man.

Having him inside her, she could feel herself building towards the impossible, rarely ever more than a faint echo for her before, but becoming stronger and stronger, pulsing through her nerve endings as he bore down upon her. God, this *never* happened to her. But it was happening. She dug her nails into his back as if she'd never let go, as sensation exploded in long, pulsating ribbons of intense pleasure that went on and on. He thrust again, once more, and gave up his release with a deep groan of satisfaction before slowly, heavily, he came down on top of her.

Ava could feel his heartbeat pounding against hers. He rolled onto his side, taking her with him, smoothing his hand along her thigh, stroking her as they both still trembled with the force of what had happened in this bed. Ava was all too aware that he was still pulsing inside her, and she was experiencing sweet aftershocks.

She buried her face in his shoulder, feeling hot and sweaty and shuddery, definitely *not* in control.

'*Mia bella*, Ava,' he said hoarsely.

His beautiful Ava.

And she was.

CHAPTER THIRTEEN

NOW WHAT?

The questions started the minute he left the bed.

Ava's eyes went a little round and glassy as she watched him move from the bed to the bathroom, his easy steps sending the musculature of his body into a stretching, look-at-me-and-learn rhythm of bunching and contraction. His naked body was truly a masterpiece of the male form.

The empty expanse of mattress stretched out around her. Instinctively she pulled the rumpled quilt over her naked body, wondering how to dial down this overwhelming need for him to hold her.

In his arms she stopped thinking, she just *felt*—and God knew she hadn't felt this good in years.

He'd given her the holy grail of sexual joy—an orgasm during sex.

Not one, Ava, but two—maybe it was three.

Was that it? Was that why she was feeling so…emotional? Because that was how she was feeling—soft and clingy and a little bit weepy.

Clearly she was a lunatic!

The bed dipped as he slid in beside her, as at ease with his nakedness as she was not.

Don't panic, her good sense told her. It was what she told her junior associates. *You have the tools to get out of this. You*

*just need time to process what's happened and a solution will
come to you...*

Oh.

Ava's eyes went wide as he encircled her with his arms and
splayed his hand in her hair, stroking her, looking at her as if
she belonged to him. He began to croon things to her in Italian. Sweet things. She knew they were sweet because of his
tone, because of the way his hand smoothed the back of her
neck, his lips brushed against her temples. His voice was so
deep, yet he spoke so softly, and he touched her as if she were
something infinitely precious.

The saliva built up in the back of her throat and Ava swallowed painfully hard.

No one had ever treated her like this. She didn't know what
to do. She couldn't let this go on. It wasn't right. It wasn't *her.*

'Gianluca?' Her voice was all scratchy, she didn't even
sound like herself.

'Luca—I want you to call me Luca, *innamorata.*' He
touched her ear with his lips and an involuntary little whim-
pering sound escaped her. She felt him smile.

'Is that the drill?' she forced out, her heart just about ham-
mering out of her chest. 'Once you get a woman into bed she
gets access to the secret name?'

If she'd thought she could cloak her anxieties in a joke it
had backfired.

It came out too snarky, too aggressive. But how could it
emerge as anything else when all she was feeling was exposed and, under that, soft and fuzzy...and terribly, terribly
vulnerable? If this man dropped her she could break into oh
so many pieces.

He said something under his breath in Italian. She knew it
was a curse because she could feel the freeze shoot through his
bigger body before so warm and enveloping against her own.
He eased himself up abruptly onto his elbow and she was instantly thrown into the even more vulnerable position of having to gaze up at him and having nowhere to go.

'Why are you doing this?'

His tone brooked no argument, and the man who had whispered sweet nothings to her was suddenly the man she had insulted.

Like a flash of light in a dark room she understood her caustic comments had hurt his pride. His very old-world Latin machismo, which made him seem impenetrable, was also what made him vulnerable to her attacks. She didn't mean to attack him. She only wanted to protect herself...

'I'm not doing anything,' she said in a small voice.

'You speak of other people while you are in my bed. You speak of me as if I am some sort of predator.'

His features were pulled taut and Ava could see she had drawn blood.

'I don't think that. I—I just wanted us to be...honest with each other. You're acting as if—'

'As if what, Ava?'

'As if I mean something to you—and how can I when we've only known one another a few days?' She brought out the big guns. 'What about Donatella?'

It took Gianluca a moment to work out who the hell Donatella was, and when he did it made even less sense. Apparently it made sense to Ava. She was glaring at him. He made a manful effort not to laugh.

'Ava, I have never been intimate with Donatella. She was a—how you say?—a prop.'

'Prop?'

'Some women—they go out, they take a man with them to hold their handbag, *si*?'

Ava looked at him suspiciously. 'I don't know any women like that.'

'Donatella carried my drink,' he supplied dryly.

'You made a woman follow you round a nightclub carrying your drink?'

'It's a euphemism, Ava. I did not want to be hassled by anyone, so I chose the lesser of the evils—Donatella.'

Ava was clearly considering this. Gianluca watched several emotions cross her face. Felt himself relax as she sank back onto the pillow.

At last. Progress.

'You must think I'm a complete idiot!'

She shot up out of the bed, dragging the sheet with her, but he wasn't having that. He grabbed it with one hand and she was left naked beside the bed. She did what he thought of as the classic pose—one arm strapped across her breasts, the other across the sweet little mop of curls at the juncture of her thighs—and backed away from the bed.

'Cara…' he said, making a placatory gesture.

'Don't you darling me, you liar!'

He stiffened and toyed with the idea of just picking her up and rolling her back into bed. But he told himself she was overwrought, and that if he wasn't careful she might hurt herself. Or him. He tried not to smile as he bounded out of bed.

She had backed herself into the wall, but not before spotting her robe. She had it on in a trice.

'How stupid do you think I am?' she snapped, securing the belt with a violent yank. 'She was beautiful. She was wearing nothing.' Her voice trembled. 'She wasn't a handbag!'

'Prop,' Gianluca amended under his breath, advancing cautiously on her.

'She wasn't that either. Is that how you're going to describe me to the next fool woman you kidnap and hold hostage? A prop?'

Ava was holding herself so rigidly it was a shock to her system when he threw back his head and laughed. The rich, raw, *edgy* sound of it hemmed her in. They stood much as they had when they begun this dance earlier.

'Why are you laughing?'

'Ava, if I don't laugh I'll throttle you.'

'I don't understand,' she said, more to herself than to him.

'I know, *cara*.' He rested one hand on the wall beside her head. Big, naked, magnificent, he made her feel entirely too girly for her own comfort. He was looking at her as if she were something he was making alterations to, and perhaps he was—cutting her right out of the picture.

Ava braced herself. This was the fall-out of giving in to the fantasy, of letting one's emotions rule. It always brought about bad things. This was what she had lectured Josh about—leading with his head, not his heart, taking only considered risks, not coming to Italy and marrying an Italian girl from an old family and *ruining his life.*

But who had ruined her life?

She was a woman who had thrown it all away seven years ago with this man, and up until a blissful five minutes ago she had been lying in his arms—only to find herself once more in the process of dismantling the tiny scrap of wonderful she'd scraped back.

'I'm sorry,' she said awkwardly. 'I shouldn't have lashed out at you.'

Gianluca wasn't really listening. He was distracted. No man would blame him. He could feel her warmth, smell the vanilla scent on her skin. He knew intimately now the softness of that skin. All women had soft skin—it was what made them wonderfully different—but with Ava it felt...*she* felt... softer...more pliant.

She just felt *better.*

He was so hard it was a special kind of torture.

He'd come back to the room and his idea had been to pull on soft old jeans and a T-shirt and do some work while he waited for Ava to wake up. He'd planned to order food. They'd eat, talk. He'd apologise for bringing her here without consulting her, she'd apologise for being a shrew and foolishly reckless, and perhaps something could be salvaged from the wreckage that was today. Perhaps he had been marginally high-handed with her, but he wasn't accustomed to women who made his life difficult.

Finding her curled up, looking so sexy-sweet in her skimpy shorts, he'd lost interest in talking. A hitherto unknown part of him had wanted to wake her up and shake her, tell her she had all the sense of a deer in headlights when it came to looking after herself with men.

She shouldn't have been curled up in some baby-doll outfit like Dorothy in a sea of poppies. She should have insisted on separate rooms. She should have shifted to another hotel. She should be halfway back to Rome! She sure as hell shouldn't trust him! If she were one of his sisters…

Which was when he'd shrugged off his sports coat, removed his watch and phone, drawn over her the quilt folded at the end of the bed to keep her warm.

He'd stood there, looking down at his handiwork, and then asked himself what the hell he thought he was doing.

When no answer had been forthcoming he'd hit the shower.

Right now he felt the same way he had when she'd uttered those immortal words, 'Maybe this isn't a good idea.' Had he *really* sprinted from the hotel, across the road, and grabbed enough protection to keep the birth rate down on a small island?

All he'd known was that he needed a chemist, needed condoms—needed to make this right for her.

It had only been when he saw her, wrapped up in that robe, looking fearful, that he'd recognised he needed to slow this down, coax her back out into the open. It had almost killed him, but taking the time to dismantle Ava's protective mechanism had possibly been one of the most erotic encounters of his life.

He wasn't going to make any sudden moves now.

'Will you answer a question?' He made sure he held her eyes seriously, hard as it was not to let his gaze drift down.

She was looking up at him, all her anxiety stamped on her expression.

'I guess I don't have a choice,' she said begrudgingly.

He almost smiled. 'Ava, you've always had a choice. You continually exercise it. You exercised it right into our bed, and now you want to pretend I have once more taken advantage of you when we both know this was what you wanted from the moment I offered you my services.'

'Services?'

She gave a start as he leaned down and brushed his mouth against her ear, 'Gigolo, escort, servicer of women.'

He drew back a little, enough to see that her lashes had drifted down, her lush mouth was quivering. She looked softened, delicious.

'Is that the fantasy you want?' he murmured over those full lips. 'Do you want me to be those things for you? Because I will do it, Ava. I'll be whatever you want me to be in this bed. But don't ask me not to be tender with you—don't ask me not to be passionate, to pretend this isn't important to you.'

'How do you know it's important to me?' Her voice was husky, her eyes downcast.

'Because...' he bent a finger around the edge of the robe '...my little porcupine...' he nudged it down until the shadowy cleft between her breasts came into view '...otherwise you wouldn't be curled up so tight right now all I can see is bristles. Ah, look—there it is.' He dragged the robe open and spread his hand over her stomach. 'Your velvety little belly,' he said, and felt the muscles in her stomach contract beneath his hand.

Ava felt the muscles in her pelvis do a similar dance, but if her insides hadn't been trembling from his declaration of intent—*to be tender, to be passionate*—she would never have nestled a little closer. Any awkwardness she felt was far outweighed by unhappiness with her own behaviour and trying to make sense of his. This man had not been careless with her feelings, she marvelled. He had, in fact, been careful and incredibly tender.

'I told you—a porcupine is a rodent,' she mumbled, moaning as he pressed his mouth softly, coaxingly to hers.

'You haven't answered my question.' He nibbled on her bottom lip.

Ava suspected she might pass out from anticipation.

'Ask me, then.' Her voice was full of longing.

'Why did you come to Rico's the other night?'

'I wanted to see if you'd changed.' She hesitated before throwing herself over the cliff. 'I wanted to spend time with you.'

He didn't seem surprised. He pressed a kiss to the corner of her mouth.

'*Si*, and why do you think I brought you here, hmm?'

Could it be that simple with a man as complicated as this?

Once again Gianluca Benedetti had taken her assumptions and sent them scattering like marbles.

She didn't have the energy to go chasing after them.

Instead she put her hands on his shoulders as he kissed the soft seam of her mouth, parted her lips. He stroked his tongue along the inner curve of her bottom lip. He *seduced* her mouth. He was the most *beautiful* kisser and when he was inside her he made her see stars.

Ava gave a little sigh and heard the rumble of a chuckle in his chest.

Yes, she was a pushover—and he knew he had her in the palm of his hand.

They emerged into the sunny street in front of the hotel around noon the next day.

Gianluca, showered and shaved and completely energised, looked incredible in a simple pair of dark trousers and one of those shirts he wore that seemed to be tailored to his powerful body.

He held her hand and walked right past the posse of pretty girls who yesterday had taken up so much of his time. Ava glanced at them and hoped her little smile wasn't too smug.

As he moved ahead of her to open the car door she caught her reflection in the mirrored surface of the window and knew beyond doubt that she had to purchase some new clothes.

Gianluca had said nothing about her trousers this morning, and she'd picked her girliest top—a short-sleeved cotton blouse with a scooped neckline. But if clothes maketh the woman they didn't reflect at all how she was feeling.

The shiny black Italian sports car shot out into the traffic, with Gianluca driving with the insouciance for which the Italians were famous—one hand on the wheel, the other playing with her hair, as if he couldn't stop touching her.

Ava's heart was pounding like a bird gone crazy in its cage.

She wanted to tell him how different this was for her—the Amalfi coast, driving in a sports car with her lover...*her lover*... Nobody back home would believe it.

A flutter of nerves swept through her. There were so many things that could go wrong.

Heck, she didn't believe this—not after the long hours she'd worked back in Sydney, the routine that had become her safety zone in an unsafe world. How had she managed to break out of that?

But she didn't feel unsafe with Gianluca. As they drove in this mad way past scooters and pedestrians and other gazillion-dollar sports cars her sense of unreality was Technicolor, but the command of the man beside her, not only over the car but his environment, was reassuring.

Gianluca Benedetti...maybe not so much playboy of the western world...maybe not at all... She looked at him with soft eyes. Maybe the man to get a crazy lady out of a fix.

'If you keep looking at me like that, *tesoro*,' he growled, 'we won't be getting where we're going.'

'And where *are* we going?'

'I thought a little touristing around the coast. There are some pretty sights I'd like to show you.'

'I'd like that too, but—'

How did she broach this? *I need to stop at some boutiques because all the clothes in my suitcase look like I've just stepped out of a business-is-us catalogue!*

'But...*tesoro*?'

'Can I have an hour? To myself?'

He gave her a curious look. 'You will not run off?' he asked, quite seriously.

'No!' Ava shot back just as seriously. 'Why would you think that?'

He grinned. 'Just checking.'

She relaxed and felt foolish. She wasn't used to this kind of banter, although she could quickly grow used to it. Her heart felt light and fluttery in her chest, as if she'd run a race and stopped and her heart didn't know it yet.

'Where should I drop you? When should I pick you up?'

Ava bit her lip. She wanted clothes—except she didn't know where to begin looking.

'Ava?'

She scanned the road, spotted some well-dressed women coming out of a shop with bags. *Bingo!*

'Anywhere here,' she instructed nonchalantly.

He grinned at her, as if she hadn't fooled him in the least, and double-parked.

'Are you sure I'm not wanted?'

He was, but she needed to do this herself. How embarrassing to ask a man to shop for her because she didn't have the first clue about what really suited her.

She had no doubt Gianluca was an expert, but the thought of him with a bevy of other far more fashion-conscious women before her wasn't something she wanted to dwell on.

'Come back in an hour.' That should give her enough time. She hoped.

As the sports car shot off once more into the traffic she felt a pang of regret, but she needed to do this for herself.

The stores seemed uniformly ordinary—and then she entered a boutique where instantly she saw what she was looking for. A long pale blue silk dress with an overlay of gossamer material embroidered with tiny blue forget-me-nots. As a little girl she had missed out on having a mother who liked to dress her up. She'd grown up in jeans and T-shirts, a real tomboy, not through preference but necessity.

This was the sort of dress she'd always thought was too girly for her even as she'd admired the look on other women.

Ignoring the price tags, Ava finally walked out with three bags, laden with her purchases. She was feeling better about her body and it gave her more confidence, trying on clothes that suited her. She made a few more purchases down the road, ditching her trousers for good and feeling much freer in a pair of white capris.

She spotted the sports car in the traffic and waved a bag at him.

Even an hour away from him and she felt her heart expand when she dived into the car. He was looking at her as if checking she was in one piece.

'Shopping? I should have guessed.'

'What do you mean?' she asked uneasily as she strapped herself in.

'Women and shopping.'

She relaxed. 'Oh, yes. That old chestnut. You know, studies have shown—'

He leaned over and kissed her.

'Oh.' She gazed back at him. 'That was nice.'

'You look beautiful,' he said, and he wasn't looking at her new capris.

'I just picked up a few things more suited to the coast,' she wittered.

He was looking at her and she couldn't take her eyes off him. A horn blasted at them from the road but Gianluca continued to stare.

'What?' she asked self-consciously.

'I was thinking,' he said slowly, 'I was in a hurry the other day. I almost didn't stop in at Nero's.'

'Nero's?'

'The coffee bar in Rome. I would have missed you—*this*.' He reached out and stroked the line of her cheek, down around the curve of her jaw.

Unaccountably Ava's eyes filled with tears. 'But you didn't miss me,' she said huskily.

'Then why are you crying, *tesoro*?'

Ava gave a self-conscious little laugh. 'I don't know.'

But she did. Her heart felt full to overflowing. He wasn't anything like the way she'd made him in her head—the self-defensive picture she'd created of a spoiled, privileged aristo-crat who didn't care about the women he slept with, only the conquests he made. He wasn't arrogant either. He just pos-sessed confidence in who he was, what he could do. Travelling with him, she felt incredibly safe and also relaxed.

All of her life *she* had been the one to take charge.

It was nice knowing she didn't have to.

He would take care of it.

The fact he expected to take care of it should have lifted her hackles, but it was difficult to begrudge him a role he as-sumed so naturally.

'Where will we go now?' she asked.

He gave her a supremely masculine smile. 'My turn to sur-prise you.'

CHAPTER FOURTEEN

'No, I COULDN'T—I can't. It's too much, Gianluca.'

'On the contrary. It's perfect.' He held the necklace, with its tiny tourmalines, green beryls, amethysts, pink sapphires and diamonds delicately wrought through a white gold chain, against her throat.

The jeweller in the exclusive little shop hovered discreetly in the background.

Ava was all too conscious of their audience—until Gianluca's shoulders blocked them out and he bent his head close to hers.

'Let me spoil you, *tesoro*,' he said, his eyes intent on hers.

'But I don't need you to buy things for me,' she answered. 'I have my own money.'

His mouth twitched. 'It is not the cost, Ava, it is the sentiment.'

She looked anxiously at the divine glittering string he hung before her and the thought flittered through her mind that it was a very expensive piece of rope she might easily hang herself on.

'Then it is a no?' he said, with that infinitesimal Latin shrug.

She wanted it so badly. Not because it was beautiful—although it was—but because he wanted her to have it. And he was being so sweet in letting her have her way although it disappointed him. He wasn't pushing it on her, and he could have no idea how good that made her feel.

Gianluca always gave her a choice, and after a lifetime of struggling and fighting to make her own choices, to have her voice heard, it was a true gift well beyond the glitter of an obscenely priced piece of jewellery.

'No.' She laid her hand on his arm. When he gave her a quizzical look she smiled and blurted out. 'I mean, yes. Yes, I want you to spoil me. If you want to.'

She'd officially handed in her Miss Independent, Miss Stand Alone card in at that moment, but Gianluca didn't seem to see the significance. He merely placed the necklace back in its box and with a barely discernible nod of his head had the jeweller and three members of his staff transferring the tiny purchase to an exquisite box.

As they emerged into the bright day after the hushed, strategically lit environs of the jeweller's Ava said, a little haplessly, 'But we left it behind.'

'No, *cara*, it will be delivered to the hotel. I didn't think you would want to carry it around all day in your handbag. Am I right?'

'No, of course not,' she muttered, feeling a little foolish. Why didn't she know these things? And now Gianluca knew she didn't have a clue.

He was the first man who had ever bought her jewellery. Not unexpectedly her mind shot to the little engagement ring she had secreted away in her suitcase. She had bought it in preparation for Bernard's proposal from an estate jewellers near her office, on her own.

She'd forgotten it in all the excitement.

Unease formed a stagnant pool in her stomach. She didn't want to think about the woman who had made that purchase, the woman who had seen nothing wrong in shelling out for their holiday *and* the ring, as if by paying for everything she could control what happened.

'You are really very sweet,' he said, putting his arm around her.

Ava disliked public displays of affection. She disliked anything that drew attention to her, so someone could say, *Look at her—what's wrong with her?* but her judgement seemed out of place at this moment, with this man…and Italy seemed to be full of canoodling couples. In fact love seemed to be a part of the public display along with dressing up and that charming custom *passeggiata*—walking every evening through the town simply to be seen.

'So are you,' she said, resting her head against his shoulder.

'I am sweet, *tesoro*?' He sounded amused.

'Yes, you always have been. I remember—' She broke off, aware she had broken her own rule not to speak about seven years ago.

But it was too late. He bent his head close to hers. 'You remember…?'

'When you were twenty-three. When we first met.' She touched his chest with her hand. 'You were so gentle, kind and sensitive, and yet strong. I felt safe with you.'

'Tesoro,' he said, capturing her hand in his and bringing it to his lips, 'you must never tell an Italian man he is *sensitive*. It just won't do.'

'I think you were—are.' She could feel that heavy weight of seven years lifting off her chest.

'If it pleases you to think so, then I'm glad,' he said neutrally.

But she sensed his resistance. He was more than simply uncomfortable with the description.

Cautiously Ava reached up and touched his jaw, running her fingertips lightly over the incipient stubble.

'It is a nuisance,' he said in a low voice, capturing her hand. 'I need to shave twice a day. Even then I will probably mark your soft skin.'

'No,' Ava said with feeling. 'I like it. I—' She broke off.

A wave of embarrassment swept through her and she didn't know what to say. She was standing in the middle of a busy street, on the other side of the world from where she had always lived, in the arms of this amazing man, saying out loud all sorts of things she would usually only whisper to her pillow, and he was listening to her and looking at her with those eyes as if...as if...

'What else do you like?' he prompted.

'I like *you*,' she said, wondering what on earth had got into her.

'*Si*, this did occur to me,' he said as he angled her towards the car, 'but I didn't like to push my luck.'

They drove the winding coastal road out of Positano. They drank limoncello and ate clams for lunch on a terraced restaurant looking out over the bay at Amalfi. They walked through the town and in the early evening strolled with half the inhabitants along the waterfront.

Gianluca had found he wanted to know everything about her.

Where she'd gone to school. Too many to count.

What was her first job? Sweeping up hair clippings in a hair salon.

Her favourite colour? Blue. Her favourite song? Anything with Billie Holliday singing it.

She'd laughed then and asked some questions of her own.

Where had he gone to school? A military academy, aged eight.

Maybe the Twenty Questions wasn't such a hot idea, he realised now, as the smile was wiped off Ava's face.

'Eight?' she repeated.

'It is how it is done in my family, *cara*. All Benedetti males have attended the same military academy for five generations.'

'Is *done*?'

'*Was* done. As I don't intend to have children the question for me is moot. But my sisters have not followed the custom with their male children.'

'No?' Her voice sounded a little hollow.

Gianluca recognised stony ground when he stood on it. Was she referring to his sisters or his comment about himself?

'You have sisters?'

Si, definitely about him.

'Two—four nephews, two nieces.' He tried not to look uncomfortable by tugging on the neck of his shirt.

'You don't like children?'

'Sure. I love kids.'

Ava regarded him with those sea-green eyes and he braced himself for the feeling of annoyance and sheer frustration a woman badgering him on this topic always aroused.

'Hmm,' she said.

It was all she said. Swishing her hair over her shoulder, she turned to look out over the water.

Just *hmm*?

Inferno, what was that supposed to mean? He didn't have to explain himself. It was a long, boring story—*Dio*, he'd told it to himself so many times even *he* was bored with it! But perhaps Ava should hear it so that she understood, so that she didn't make any plans involving him...

'This is magical. I can see why people turn out in the evening to promenade,' she said unexpectedly, turning up eyes made soft by the light. 'We should go out on the water tomorrow.'

Tomorrow he had planned on meeting with some investors.

'Unless you've planned something else?'

Could a woman look more guileless? All her anticipation and uncertainty flickered in those few words.

What could he say?

'Anything you desire, Ava *mio*.'

The next day he took her out in a motorboat along the coast, around the Galli Islands. The day after they drove into the Lattari Mountains cradling the Amalfi Coast.

A light rain began to fall and, hand in hand, they ran to shelter in a local church. In the dim incense-scented light he couldn't take his eyes off her. He didn't know what it was—perhaps it was the coastal light—but she seemed to shimmer in the gloom. Her dark shoulder-length cloak of hair, her pearly skin, the deep pink of her mouth—all hot colours on a rainy day. She rested against him, looking out at the rain, with his hands hooked around her waist, his head resting against hers.

The weight of her was perfect.

She smelled like vanilla and cloves.

She smelled like Ava.

'Do you see that hill?' She pointed dead ahead. 'It looks like a rabbit's head.'

He couldn't see the rabbit.

'Si, *innamorata*. A fluffy little bunny.'

She eyed him wryly.

'And over there—the forest. That's a boot.'

'*Si*, a boot.'

'I made that one up to see if you were humouring me! And it's not a forest—it's a wood.'

She shoved her shoulder into his chest playfully and then gave a little cry of delight.

'Oh, look—is that a fox?'

The whisk of red across the pasture was indeed a fox.

He felt her thrill and realised that although he knew this area like the back of his hand, from boyhood summers with his maternal grandparents, looking at it through her eyes made him feel as if he was seeing this place for the first time.

He didn't have the heart to tell her that the fox was probably on its way to gobble up any real rabbits foolish enough to be darting around in the rain. She was a true city girl. She was…

Making him crazy. *Pazzo.* Why was he discussing furry animals, in a church in a little village no one had ever heard of, when he had a hotel suite waiting for them? He wasn't a tour guide, and he sure as hell didn't think foxes were something to be delighted over rather than thought of as the vermin they were.

He'd tell her that in a minute. He'd drag her out of here and they'd make a run for the car, rain or no rain, and drive all the way back to Positano at speed. And when they got to the hotel he'd strip her clothes off her and do what a *sensible* man would be doing with a beautiful woman—not hunkering down in churches on a day custom-made for more adult indoor activity.

Then he'd get around to organising their transport south, because tomorrow was D-Day and all he'd been doing was dragging his feet round these tourist traps for days.

She turned in his arms and looked up, her eyes shining. 'I've never seen a fox before—at least not so close.'

'*Si*, they're shy little animals,' he found himself saying. 'You have to play your hand carefully around them...no sudden moves.'

Which was when, instead of whisking her off for some debauchery, as he had done a hundred times before with other women, he bent his head and kissed her soft, delicious mouth. He forgot about D-Day and tourist traps and the idiocy of delighting in foxes and accepted he was possibly the luckiest *bastardo* in the world.

In town, he let her out to run another one of her mysterious errands, idling the car above the waterfront. He caught sight of her coming across the grass, the sun as bright here as it had been banished by cloud cover in the hills, shining on her chocolate hair.

She looked *Italian*—there was no other word for it—in her simple button-front sundress. She even wore it sliding slightly over one shoulder, with the top two buttons undone over her cleavage and the bottom three buttons undone to reveal a portion of her long thighs with each step as the skirt opened over her knees. She looked happy and earthy and incredibly sexy, and Gianluca became aware his wasn't the only pair of eyes on her.

As he got out of the car a piercing wolf whistle had her looking around, and him looking too, to hunt the perpetrator down.

He knew he hadn't stopped thinking about her since she'd walked back into his life. He knew he would never forget her as she had been last night, wearing the string of pretty stones—wearing *only* the pretty stones—in his bed.

Even before she'd accepted them, as he'd held them up against her pale throat in the jeweller's, watched her breasts below her clavicles rise and fall, he'd seen them draped on her naked.

He'd also seen the tremble in her hand as she took the string from him, and the vexation that had sent her dark brows together as she wrestled with her conscience.

There could be a hundred and one reasons why a woman would not accept a gift from a man. Ava's reason had been as transparent as those green eyes of hers. The gift meant something to her.

As you wanted it to, idiota.

He shifted uneasily on his feet. It wasn't a pledge...it wasn't a *ring*. It was just a token—no, more than that. It was a gesture—a sign of his esteem...his affection.

And why shouldn't he feel affectionate towards her? It was easy to stumble into putting labels on things, on feelings—and, yes, he *did* have feelings for her. Fairly strong feelings.

Perhaps he always had.

It didn't mean this was anything beyond his experience...although it was.

She was.

He watched Ava bending down to pet a small dog. She was speaking to the owner, her face turned up like a sunflower.

What would she think about his plan?

If she said no, if she insisted on continuing with this ridiculous excursion to Ragusa...

She stood up and turned her head.

Her smile made his heart turn over in his chest.

It crashed through him as he stood on a pavement in Positano, amidst scooters and tourists eating gelato and a hundred other peripherals that had never touched his everyday life—until this woman stepped into it and brought it into his world.

The simple happiness of being with this woman.

The way she made him feel.

'Ava.'

She turned to him, oblivious to what had just occurred in his world, and said, 'Luca, this gentleman breeds Lhasa Apsos—'

He framed her face with his big hands.

'Come back to Rome with me.'

Her mouth opened. No sound. But her eyes went soft and round and a little soulful.

'No family. No Ragusa. No pretence, Ava. Just you and me. Say yes, *innamorata*.'

She didn't hesitate.

'Yes,' she said.

He flew them back to Rome.

A small jet from Naples, in deference to Ava's needs.

They shot down the highway in his beloved Lamborghini Aventador roadster at dusk. He dropped the speed as they hit the drowsy late afternoon streets of the city he loved and everything became larger than life—the crumbling façades of old buildings, the ruins among the new that was Rome.

It was the old that hung like a millstone around his neck.

But *this* was new. This surging feeling—this certainty of purpose about a woman.

He didn't want to share her with his family. He didn't want her to have to deal with her brother.

To this end he'd arranged for two hundred red roses to land on his mother's lap tomorrow morning by way of apology, and Ava had phoned her brother.

'He asked me to put in a good word with you,' she'd said in a bemused fashion when she had emerged from the bedroom with her phone.

'You told him we were together?'

Even now he couldn't believe he'd been tactless enough to say it.

Ava's expression had neutralised in an instant. 'I didn't know it was a secret.'

No, not a secret—but how to explain that in the past the women in his fishbowl world had appreciated his discretion?

This wasn't like that. It wasn't a liaison. It wasn't anything either of them should be ashamed of.

He didn't intend to hide her away in the *palazzo*. He hadn't exactly formulated a plan, but he wanted to show her Rome, and naturally that would include meeting people—people who mattered to him—introducing her as…as…

He looked over at her now. She was scrolling through her phone, checking the e-mails from her business.

He cleared his throat. 'Ava—'

Ava said a rude word.

'Cara…?'

'Stop the car.'

When he continued to drive she wailed, *'Please*, Benedetti!'

It was the please that worked. Braking and pulling over, he barely had the car to a standstill before she sprang out.

Swearing fairly colourfully himself Gianluca leapt out after her, stalking around to where she stood with one hand on her hip, the other waving her phone at him.

'Guess who spotted us on a celebrity gossip site on the internet? *Guess?'*

He hadn't seen this side of Ava since—well, since she'd been in his bed. All her fire had been directed one way, and now it was going another. He couldn't say his life had been dull since her advent into it.

'The Pope?'

'My personal assistant! Do you know what this means? Everyone in the bloody office is talking about me and "the Italian Prince"—like I'm Mary Donaldson or something.'

'Cosa?'

She waved the phone again. 'Mary Donaldson from Tasmania—married the Crown Prince of Denmark. Big wedding. He cried. Australia finally got itself a royal!' Ava shook her head. 'You really need to pay attention to the news.'

Gianluca considered telling her he'd been at the wedding, but there were more important things under consideration.

'You are unhappy because your employees know you have a personal life?'

'This is hardly a personal life. Seedy is how it looks!'

Gianluca stilled and looked at her. She stood with one hand on her hip. The white capri pants showed off her long legs. The pale blue T-shirt moulded to her like a second skin.

It was impossible to imagine her in those ugly black trousers, that mumsy silk blouse, with her mouth drawn into a tight, suspicious line. *Go away. I don't want you.*

She might be steaming at him, but she seemed to be having a good time and she was undeniably sexy doing it.

This thing between them had softened her, tempered her, and it had touched him too…

He was happy, and he had no idea how it had happened.

'You'll have to fix this,' she said imperiously.

'Fix it?'

'Yes—issue some sort of statement, make up a story like you said you would about us being related and it being some sort of trick of the photo…'

Gianluca believed this was called being hoist with his own petard.

He strode back to the car.

'What are you doing?' she called after him.

He gunned the engine and Ava moved *rapidamente*, sliding in beside him. She barely had her seatbelt on when he took off, damn sure of one thing—this needed sorting out once and for all.

'What are we doing here?'

Ava was aware her voice was a little shrill but she'd had a fright. The e-mail from PJ had shaken her. The knowledge that people were talking about her, that those photographs were floating around in the ether, had thrown her. She didn't know why it bothered her so much, but suddenly what had seemed romantic felt entirely out of her control.

She'd never had romance in her life, never allowed herself to be vulnerable enough to a man to let her guard down. Now she had and look what had happened—people were talking about her.

She could guess what they were saying…that she was just the latest in a long line…

It made her feel unimportant to him, and this less than what she'd thought it was.

And, really, what was she doing with this man? Where did she think this was going?

Ava, you need to be sensible.

This last was the voice of her past. The little girl who'd had the responsibility for both her mother and her baby brother on her shoulders from far too young an age.

Gianluca had her door open and he took her hand, none too gently.

'Benedetti, I will not go any further until—'

He almost yanked her off her feet and she had to struggle to keep up with him.

The café he took her into was crowded. It was also terrifyingly elegant, and Ava felt under-dressed—especially as heads turned.

'Gianluca, *darling*!'

This seemed to come from a variety of women. Her already shaky confidence did a nosedive.

'Where have you been, my friend?'

A man rose from his table but Gianluca didn't stop, didn't deviate from his course.

Ava tried to loosen his grip, but now he had a hand around her waist, was propelling her in front of him as they were shown by the busboy to a prominent table.

He pulled out her chair.

'Sit down, Ava.'

She sat, too astonished to do anything else. She looked

around and wished she hadn't. People were staring at them. 'How can you just walk in and get a table? Why are we here?' she hissed, all the while trying to keep a social, nothing-to-see-here-people expression on her face.

She tried not to react as she recognised a film director. Undeniably this was a glamorous crowd, out to be seen.

Gianluca leaned across the table and took her hands.

There was a sudden lull in conversation at the tables around them.

'What are you doing?'

He gave her a warm smile. 'If I kiss you now, Ava, it will mean we are an item. Everyone will be talking about us—all of Roman society. You will be the girl who has taken Prince Benedetti's heart. So think carefully before you answer me. We can have a drink together, some food, and nothing needs to change. Do you understand?'

She found herself nodding, then shaking her head. *What was he saying?*

'But I would like to kiss you, Ava *mio*, if you would let me.'

She understood that bit.

And, gazing into his eyes, she began to understand the rest.

Almost as if in a dream she moistened her lips, dropped her lashes, softened her mouth in readiness.

She felt his smile as one hand curled around the back of her head and his mouth met hers in a kiss so tender, so sincere, she could only read it as a pledge.

A light smattering of applause broke out at the tables around them.

'Now you are mine,' he said, with his smile against her lips.

He showed her Rome.

He introduced her to his home, his friends, his life.

He took her to restaurants, to theatres, to parties.

They ate together, slept together, and made love as if they'd just discovered the newness of the world and wanted to celebrate creation.

What did it mean?

Ava didn't know and it was killing her—the sense that around the corner waited something large and ferocious, something she couldn't define or defeat.

She stood now in the studio of one of Rome's leading couturiers, being fitted into a strapless midnight blue gown of such sumptuous scale Ava couldn't imagine an event grand enough as its backdrop. But she had trusted Gianluca when he'd explained the Black & White Ball, this year in aid of a breast cancer charity, was one of the highlights of the social calendar. It was an international affair and ballgowns were a requirement.

This dress was certainly going to make a statement. She only hoped the right kind.

She nervously voiced her fears to the three women circling her.

The seamstress at her feet looked up through the folds of satin and said, 'This is a fantasy dress, *signorina*. All you need is the confidence to carry it off.'

'You have the height,' said one of the others.

Ava translated the fulsome gesture from the third towards her breasts with her schoolgirl Italian. 'And the necessary *vavoom*.'

As she stepped out into the street in her civvies she wanted to pinch herself. These had been the most magical, wonderful, inspiring four weeks of her life. If nothing ever happened to her again half as good she would treasure this time, keep it locked up in her heart always against the hard winter when she didn't have love in her life.

Because she suspected it *was* love. As she slid into the plush confines of the limo Gianluca had put at her disposal she acknowledged the truth. She might not have had much of it in her life, but she knew what it looked like when it arrived.

CHAPTER FIFTEEN

ACROSS TOWN, GIANLUCA was in the elegantly appointed offices of Benedetti International from where he ran the world, as Ava put it.

He only half listened to his lawyer on the other end of the line as he stood at the window, looking down on the busy square below.

Everywhere he looked there were couples, old and young. Even the pigeons roosting outside the window came in a pair.

Two generations ago his family's marriages were still being arranged. It was different now. His father had chosen his mother of his own free will—the beautiful Sicilian model Maria Trigoni, who at that time had had her own small moment of fame in a Fellini film. Fidelity had not been high on either of his parents' minds when they made that merger. Prince Ludovico had wanted a beautiful woman on his arm and Maria had liked the title.

At thirty, Gianluca was very accustomed to women who liked the title. They liked the idea of having *Principessa* dangling in front of their name. They saw the *palazzo* in the middle of Rome, the house in Regent's Park, London, the Manhattan apartment, and started ordering monogrammed napkins for the wedding.

All his life he had imagined that when he came to choose a wife his choices would be constrained by the world in which he moved. Watching his parents tear each other apart had not encouraged him to look beyond the highly stratified and stage-managed relationships he'd engaged in all of his life.

Until now.

In Positano they had discussed their work lives—his offices in Rome, New York and London. The deals that put him over the edge, the rush of trade that she so well understood. Ava had spoken about her difficulties with clients—a mining magnate who'd insisted on meeting with her when he came to Sydney at his gym, so she ended up on a stationary cycle talking about his hedge fund. Worse, he was competitive and had insisted she match his rpm.

'Do I *look* like a cyclist?' she'd asked.

'You, *cara*, you look like a goddess.'

But now they were in Rome, spending all their time together, and the conversations were deepening. Last night in bed he'd told her about his childhood fascination with flight, his godfather's encouragement, his father's impatience. Deeply private things.

'He didn't want you to fly?'

Ava had been propped up in his arms, her head beside his. She'd been wearing that little ice-blue lace thing he'd bought her.

'My father wanted me to come into the family business—the banking group. It was all he wanted for me. He saw the planes as a hobby, at worst, a distraction.'

'But it was your passion.'

'It meant nothing,' he said bluntly. 'My entire upbringing was based on discipline—being tough, being a man. What I wanted didn't much come into it.'

'Yet you pushed for it? For what you wanted?'

'Si.' He had noticed how fierce Ava looked in that moment. 'You had to fight for something too, Ava *mio*?'

'Working class girl, left school at fifteen,' she'd said, lifting that stubborn chin of hers. 'Damn right I did.'

He'd kissed her then, and made love to her until the memory of how hard he'd had to push for what he wanted and the consequences of that had been wiped out by a deep sense of having something special at last within his grasp. Something far more important than his passion for flight, his ability with the stock market, all the decisions right or wrong that he'd taken in life. Something that had nothing to do with duty or the family name.

Lying in his arms afterwards, she'd told him more about her business back home—a firm that turned over multi-million-dollar accounts—and how she'd drudged full-time to put herself through university in a variety of jobs, the three years she'd worked for other companies as a broker, setting up her connections as ruthlessly as a Roman emperor assembling legions, until at the incredibly tender age of twenty-eight she'd taken the plunge and set up her own firm.

He had told her in turn one of his other secrets—the breaks he took in Anguilla in the Caribbean, at the place he owned down there, the hideaway nobody knew about. And once he'd told her he'd found himself wanting to show it to her. When he'd asked her if she had somewhere she went to drop out of sight for a time she'd admitted it had been a while since she'd been on a holiday.

'Define "a while"?' he'd teased, kissing her neck.

'Never.'

'You've *never* been on a holiday?'

'I'm here now, and I came here for Josh's wedding. I've travelled for business, but just for me, getting away from it all—no.'

She'd looked embarrassed, but also defiant, as if daring him to pass comment.

A knot had formed at the base of his throat.

That knot was still there now.

His lawyer said intrusively, 'If we move now we'll have them over a barrel.'

He flicked his thoughts back to the present. 'Then we move. Let me know when it's done.'

He turned away from the window and the display of happy couples everywhere.

Thinking about Ava, he focussed not on the future but on the now, where he was most comfortable—on the rather narrow, unrelieved tedium she'd described—and it galvanised him.

Certamente he'd take her to Anguilla. He'd take her around the world if her heart desired it. But right now he wanted to play hooky with her. Take the day off. Stand on top of the world.

But first he had an important errand to run. He got his assistant on the line and asked her to notify the bank that he'd be paying a visit to the vault in around half an hour.

He picked her up in the Aventador and headed for Palatine Hill.

They took a picnic with them and in the late afternoon climbed through the ruins of the imperial palace complex, looking down over the Circus Maximus.

Ava had fallen quiet when they'd first arrived. It wasn't the spot they'd come to seven years ago, but there was the same view of the city, the long grass, the pencil pines. Not that he was in a hurry to rake over *those* coals. Whenever he remembered waking that morning to reach for her, only to grasp emptiness, anger rolled through him—and he didn't want to be angry with her.

Not today.

'When my grandparents were courting they came up here,' he said. 'My grandmother was an archaeologist and very much obsessed with this place.' He found himself adding, 'It was a love match, not at all arranged.'

'Does that make a difference?' asked Ava, picking her way over the rocky ground.

'If it had been arranged there would have been respectful afternoons at one another's parents' houses, chaperoned trips to the opera and summer on the coast where the two families would discuss terms.'

'All so two strangers could marry?'

'Not strangers, *cara*. All the families knew one another. I should add that my grandmother came from another old family, so it wasn't a difficult concept for the two sets of parents to accept.'

Ava didn't say anything.

He cleared his throat. 'It's somewhat different now.'

'I guess Josh came as a bit of a shock, then,' she said out of the blue.

Josh who? His normally razor-sharp brain took a few seconds to register the name.

'Your brother,' he concluded reluctantly, aware that the afternoon was going places he hadn't intended it to. 'I won't lie and say there was universal joy, but that had less to do with him not being Italian and more to do with his ability to provide for Alessia.'

'*Provide* for her?' Ava gave a nervous laugh. 'Last time I looked this was the twenty-first century, Benedetti, or hadn't you noticed?'

Si, he'd noticed. If it wasn't she'd be over his shoulder and halfway back to the *palazzo*, where she'd stay locked up.

'I forgot...' she glanced back at him over her shoulder '—you live in a cave.'

'A *palazzo*,' he drawled, 'but close.'

She needed to accept he was a man who would look after her, that he was not one of these excuses for men she had been putting up with—this brother of hers, who clearly had so little regard for his sister that this was the first time in seven years she had been mentioned. Her ex-boyfriend, whom Gianluca hoped one day to cross paths with. The man who had left her fearful of intimacy—so fearful, in fact, that she'd fought him like a wildcat all the way down that mountain at Positano.

His woman now. She would never be that woman again.

He followed the sway of her hips as she stepped carefully over the broken ground.

He heard himself say, 'Look around you, Ava. There have

been people living on the Palatino for a thousand years, and I'm sure back then, as now, a man's worth could be judged on his ability to protect his family.'

Ava stopped and drew herself tall, but didn't turn around. 'A woman protects her family too.'

'Naturally.' He stepped up close behind her. 'You protected your brother all his life. But at some point he had to stand on his own two feet, Ava.'

'How do you know I protected him?'

'You told me here, on that night, about your mother's fragile mental health. How you worried for her, how you'd had to puzzle out the best care for her as she lay dying, how guilty you felt, how alone. And I remember wondering why you didn't have any help.'

Ava's turned around, her face pale.

'I had no idea you were the groom's sister. If I'd known I would have sorted him out for you.'

'Sorted him out?'

'Reorganised his priorities. A man should be responsible for his mother and sister.'

Her mouth formed a tight line. 'I don't need anyone to be responsible for me, Benedetti.'

He understood her resistance. She wouldn't be Ava if she didn't struggle against any incursion on her independence. He understood that too.

'I get it. You don't like my brother. You think he's beneath your high-and-mighty family. Well, newsflash—I wasn't happy about the damn wedding either. I did my best to talk him out of it. I told him he was making a big mistake. Alessia was far too young, and so was he, and I knew your family didn't approve. Your mother—' She broke off, pursing her lips.

'My mother was most vocal, I understand. I suspect she was not kind to you.'

She turned away. 'I don't wish to say anything critical about your mother.'

'Then allow me.' He turned her in his arms. 'She's a manipulative woman who likes everything to revolve around her. She is also highly emotional and not above using a little blackmail to get what she wants. My sisters act as her ladies-in-waiting, so I imagine the women of my family made your life miserable.'

'They were not welcoming,' Ava said tightly. 'That's why I elected to move to a hotel.'

He had to ask. 'Where were you staying?'

Ava dropped her gaze to the base of his throat.

'The Excelsior,' she said in a tight voice.

The same hotel he'd picked her up from last month. The same hotel he'd driven past that day on his way to the hospital...

He couldn't believe it—the Excelsior!

'I stayed there all day...' She lifted her eyes to his. 'Hoping you'd call.'

She'd hoped he would call?

'How?' It burst aggressively out of him and he let go of her, because he didn't trust the strength in his hands. 'How was I supposed to call?'

She staggered back as if hit by a blast furnace.

'You didn't leave a number. But you knew who *I* was. There was nothing stopping *you*, Ava.'

She looked stricken. 'I know.'

'Not. Good. Enough.' The words stamped through his brain, made him want to pound something. He held on to the edges of his self-control as a tidal wave of anger swept everything he'd planned for this afternoon out of reach. He hadn't known until this moment how strong his feelings were.

Ava had wrapped her arms around herself. But her chin was up and she looked defiant, not scared.

'I know that too,' she said. 'But, really, what would have happened? Had you fallen head over heels in love with me? Were we going to spend the rest of our lives together? It was just a night, Luca, and I knew you'd had many just like them.

I only had that one. *One.*' Her voice cracked. 'I wanted to take it with me—intact, perfect.'

'Perfect?' He snarled. 'What was perfect about it? Casual sex with a guy you didn't know? Didn't want to know afterwards?'

She flinched, her eyes reproachful.

'Oh, and you have never done that? You have never just had sex with a woman you had no intention of seeing again?'

'Si, I have done that.' He looked into her stormy green eyes, more dark blue than green in this light, in this mood. 'But I had no intention of doing that with you.'

Ava's sharp intake of breath was the only sound, but in his head Gianluca was hearing himself on this subject for the first time.

The excited voices of a group of children coming up from below had Ava reacting first, looking around as if realising where they were. Without even glancing at him she bolted for a gate to the winding walkway that wound down to the base of the incline.

He was breathing hard by the time he reached her at the car, but it had nothing to do with the exercise. She had her arms folded and she looked murderous.

'I can't believe you would lie to me like that,' she flung at him.

Fury pumped through his veins. At himself, at his father, at this woman who demanded too much from him.

'I do not lie, I do not cheat, and *you*—' he stabbed a finger at her '—you do not run from me again!'

'So speaks Prince Benedetti, Prince of—'

'Of all he surveys—*si,* I got it the first time.'

He took hold of her elbow and jerked her around, dragging her up against him. The scent of her—vanilla and female skin—filled his senses. But the warm, fragrant softness of her body didn't remind him of all the times she had cleaved to him naked; it only served to enrage him more.

She *did* this to him. She made him crazy and furious and

then she sucker-punched him with the fact that she was a woman he would do anything for, and that just left him with nowhere to go.

He wanted her in ways that weren't just sexual—ways that would make any single man nervous—and it was beginning to make him *pazzo*...crazy.

Maybe he *was* crazy. Especially now, as he hauled her up and kissed her. He didn't make it tender or easy or any of the things he'd done with her before. He kissed her with all the wildness of his lust for her, and Ava's body sprang up against his as if this was what she had been waiting for.

A lot of things were different in both their lives. It was time to take the gloves off and see what this thing between them was made of.

He had her up against the car, her skirt worked high on her thighs, and his hand found her hot, wet welcome. She jumped and cried out when he touched her, lifting one leg to his hip, dragging him in against her, rubbing her sensitive inner thigh over his jeans, inviting what was inevitable... He knew right there and then that he had a matter of seconds to make up his mind before his body did it for him. He was a heartbeat away from freeing himself from the purgatory of denim and thrusting inside her.

He cursed, reefing away from her. They were in the middle of a car park! No one was around, but that didn't mean they couldn't have company in the next five minutes.

Ava's eyes were unfocussed, dark, and her colour was high. Her chest rose and fell as, visibly shaken, she drew her stretchy cardigan around her shoulders. Some of the buttons were loose at the top of her dress but she didn't seem to notice.

'Come on,' he said, trying to exert some control on the situation, pressing her into the car. 'We need to get out of here.'

But Ava's head was down, she looked fragile, and although he told himself it was her own fault—she'd created all this—it wasn't true.

He was just as responsible as she was for that night, and she hadn't just run from him—he'd lost her.

He'd been so caught up in what his family wanted from him he'd let this—*Ava*—go.

And maybe that was the price his father had finally exacted—not the stint in the military, or the loss of his football career. The true legacy of being a Benedetti was wanting a woman and not being able to hold on to her. Not the way he wanted to.

The small square box lay heavy inside his jacket.

Without speaking another word he put her in the car and took her home.

Ava stripped off her clothes and immersed herself under the water jets in the wet room. She found she couldn't cry, although the feeling was a pressure in her body, one she couldn't relieve. As the warm water ran down her back she didn't make any effort towards washing her hair, which had been her plan, just let the water sluice through it.

She felt fragmented—as if all the pieces of the Ava she had built up so carefully over the years not only to survive but to flourish had broken apart and she now had to work out which parts went where.

I had no intention of doing so with you.

Those words had hurt her. Because they hinted at what she suspected was true—she could have had all this seven years ago and she'd thrown it away because she'd been afraid to reach out for it and have it disappear.

The only delusion, it seemed, had been her own.

'Ava.'

He was stripped, bigger than her, muscular, his broad shoulders, narrowing to his lean hips, those long, powerful legs. His expression was intent on her.

He often shared her shower, but right now she felt too raw, too exposed to be naked in front of him. She turned towards the splashback, feeling trapped.

She wanted to weep when his hands slid over her hips. As if sex would make everything all right—more likely the emotional turmoil of this afternoon hadn't affected his attitude to that part of their relationship at all. He was a man—what did she expect? Sensitivity? Cry on another woman's shoulder for that.

Yet as he smoothed one hand around her inner thigh and the other cupped her breast, and as he played his mouth hot and teasing over the back of her neck, Ava could feel her body delighting in his touch, eager to experience this yet again.

She had never thought herself a sexual creature. She had often wondered late at night when Bernard had gone home— she had never let him stay overnight—if she had enhanced that night with Gianluca in her memory. But now she knew better. Memory couldn't supply the heat of his body, the scent of him on her skin, the hunger of his mouth, the demand, the way he stretched her with his size and his sheer stamina. Nor could it replicate the gentleness with which he held her afterwards and how supremely female she felt—replete, wanted, loved.

All illusory, of course. It was just the way you felt after good sex—*great* sex.

She'd never had great sex before, so she was bound to get confused.

Just as her body was confused now, as he turned her in his arms and heat rushed up from her sex and set her whole body alight.

'Gianluca...' she said on a sigh, her brain trying to assert itself.

They were toe to toe and his erection nudged her belly.

He kissed her, his mouth hot, wet under the spray. He tasted so good. Her fingers tried to get purchase on the hard ridges of his shoulders, slipped to his biceps, silk over steel. His physicality did it for her—the hardness of his honed body, so different from her own. His hair-roughened chest felt so good riding against the sensitive tips of her breasts.

Too easy—too easy to lose herself in this.

'Things have been too intense over the last few weeks,' he explained as his mouth roamed over her neck, her shoulders, found her nipple. His voice was slurred with lust. 'Let's just do this—this works for us, *tesoro*.'

Ava wanted to weep as he sucked her nipple into his mouth. There was so much to say. But this—for now—would do. He thought this would do.

He picked up a cloth, soaped it up and began to drag it over her until she was wobbly-kneed and leaning back against the tiles. He slid to his knees and found the soft heat between her legs. Ava shoved a fist to her mouth to stifle the scream building inside her, her other hand tangling its fingers in his hair. She pulled hard as she convulsed, and screamed anyway. He picked her up and, dripping water, took her to the bed, rolled her onto her belly and entered her from behind with a swift certainty that had her senses firing again.

He was impossibly deep inside her and she climaxed with a shocking immediacy.

His expression as he turned her over was almost feral in its wildness. There was none of the gentleness he was usually so careful to show to her, handling her as if she were somehow less robust than him, easily bruised, needed special consideration.

Ava was damn well aware she was going to have bruises tomorrow, and she didn't care.

He thrust so deeply inside her that she gasped, and then again and again, until there was no room for thought, no doubt, only the tension coiling once more, coming like an earthquake from a long way away.

Her mind orbited separately from her body as she wrapped her legs around him and clung until she was sobbing out her pleasure. He made a deep, gratified sound and then there was just their bodies joined, her heavy breathing as she lay with her head plastered to his shoulder, his harsh breathing as his chest rose and fell.

Ava slowly became aware that tension still inhabited her

body, despite the most intense orgasm of her life. Feeling unbearably heavy, she lifted herself up and rolled onto her back, gasping for breath as if she'd just run an endurance race.

She flopped her head to one side and his eyes met hers, still glowing with that intense explosion of desire she'd seen in them as he thrust inside her. It was banked down now, but it was there. Feral, hot, intensely male.

This works for us. That was what he had said. No soft words, no promises, no mention that she would be going home soon. Just, *Things have been too intense...this works for us.*

The tension pulled wire-tight and she knew she had two choices. She could kill him...or she could kill him.

'Again,' she said.

Hours later, when it was still and dark and the only sound was the cicadas through the open windows, he said slowly, 'That night we met I had a lot on my mind.'

He felt her shift but she didn't say a word.

'My father and I had had an argument the day before. God knows it didn't seem important at the time.'

'What did you argue about?' Her voice was soft.

'I had responsibilities and I was trying to evade them.'

'What sort of responsibilities?'

'Look around you, Ava. I'm a Benedetti.'

Around them was a vast bedchamber. A great empty marble fireplace, lights in sconces, frescos on the wall, heavy bed-hangings. He wondered if she understood the weight of having all this history around your shoulders.

It wasn't exactly subtle.

'I was eighteen when I graduated from the military academy and went away to the States to start an Economics degrees at MIT. My father assumed I would be using that degree to work in the family business and he turned a blind eye to my life in the US. I was almost twenty-one when I graduated and was recruited to the professional football league.'

He scrubbed his jaw where the beard was already growing in.

'Tell me about the soccer. It must have been very glamorous.'

'Sometimes. Mostly it was training and keeping my nose clean.'

'And parties, and girls...' she trailed off.

'It was a wild time,' he admitted, not about to lie to her. 'But for me it was all about the freedom. You can't know what it was like after all the years of toeing the line.'

Ava made a soft snorting sound. 'Oh, I think I can, but go on.'

'We had a confrontation the day before Alessia's wedding. I told him this was my chance and I wasn't giving it up. My father said I should be by his side at the meetings with the Agostini Banking Group. It was time I showed him I was serious. I told him they were nothing better than organised criminals, and he struck me. I said things I could never take back. I told him I hated him, that he was weak. I hated him for what he'd done to my mother and that my whole purpose in life was never to be like him.'

He pulled himself up a little straighter in the bed.

'He told me I was to put on a suit and go to Naples with him for the meeting. I laughed at him and chose instead to go to my cousin's wedding.'

'Our night,' she said softly.

'The night of the reception, the night we were together—yes, our night.'

Now there was only the sound of the cicadas. They both seemed to be holding their breaths.

'Tell me,' she said.

'He had a massive heart attack. He was only fifty-three.'

'I'm sorry.'

'I never got to take any of it back. He was under tremendous strain. He'd dug himself a hole stretching back twenty years, full of debt and corruption. The entire banking group collapsed, two of his business partners were gaoled, and most of the property was sold to meet the debts.'

'And you joined the military after all,' was all she said.

'For the honour of my family, for my father. It was what he wanted,' he said softly. 'I know it's hard to understand, and I don't entirely understand it myself, but ours was once a good name. It represented service to the state, an integrity that could not be compromised, and in two generations that had been destroyed. I wanted to build something from the ashes, and the military seemed as good a place as any to start.'

'That's why I couldn't contact you,' she said slowly. 'I rang all those numbers you gave me and only one of them, the one to your office, was connected. I guess the message was never passed on.'

Gianluca stilled. 'The media went after our family like piranhas. All the numbers were changed. You left a message, *cara*?'

'A number and my name.'

Gianluca was silent.

Ava moistened her lips. 'That's why you never came for me.'

'Came for you?'

'When I left that morning I thought you knew who I was.'

'But how, *cara*? You only gave me your given name, and even that I got wrong.'

She lifted her head, blinked at him. 'Wrong?'

'I thought you said Evie.'

'Excuse me.' She began to roll off the bed.

He caught her hand. 'Where are you going?'

Ava pulled her hand away. She grabbed her silk robe from the chair and pulled it around her nakedness.

'To get a drink.'

Gianluca had a nice range of spirits in his study, but Ava reached straight for the sherry.

He might not have known her name, but she was the one who'd got everything wrong! Making believe that night was special only to her, holding on to it in her hot little hand as if it belonged to her. Cutting him out of the picture completely.

Life had taught her to keep her feelings locked up. Her father leaving. The upheaval her mother's illness had wrought as she and Josh were farmed out to friends and neighbours.

She remembered all too well as a small girl believing her mother's assurance that their father would come back to them. As she'd grown older she had learned to rely only on what she could quantify, and she had worked hard to pull herself up out of the poverty cycle their mother's illness had put them in.

But that need to guard herself and shred reality of all illusion had done her no favours when it came to her personal relationships. Josh had fled the country to get away from her, she'd wasted two years of her life in a relationship with a man she would never love, and as for her one chance at having something truly magical—she'd destroyed it simply through fear.

She'd run when she should have stood her ground.

Cowardly Ava.

She splashed a little sherry on the sideboard.

'Ava.' His deep voice cut through the shadows.

'I'm sorry,' she said, in a voice she barely recognised as her own because it was so deep with the weight of emotions she hadn't allowed herself to feel in so long—perhaps ever. She tried to think of something else to say, but what came out again was, 'I'm sorry.'

She almost dropped the glass as he came up to her.

He took it out of her hand, lifted it to his nose. 'This won't do, Ava. *Sherry?*'

He put the glass on the sideboard and drew her into his arms.

'I'm sorry,' she said yet again.

'For what, *innamorata*?' He seemed bewildered.

'What do you think? Everything—everything you went through.'

'It's life. These things make us stronger, make us appreciate what we have in the now, don't you think?'

He wasn't only talking about his father. He was talking about them.

Not love, sex. Sex was what they had. Love might have had

a chance once—but she had thrown it away without knowing what she'd almost had.

All her life she'd picked her battles and won them. But this battle she hadn't chosen. It had come along and taken her on and she didn't know how to fight it. Then or now. So she'd lost without even knowing she'd once had a chance with her magnificent, proud lion in their own personal Colosseum.

CHAPTER SIXTEEN

THE BALLROOM WAS ALIGHT with thousands of tiny candles and four hundred people who had all paid a premium price to be here.

Ava's heart was like a trapped bird inside her, fluttering desperately to get out. She had needed help tonight to get into the dress. A hairdresser had been flown in from Paris to style her hair, and a make-up artist from Milan. The fragrance mingling with her skin had been mixed for her by a perfumer here in Rome, based on details Gianluca had provided. Nothing about tonight was natural.

'Relax, Ava,' Gianluca said softly, whirling her in his arms. 'You are the most beautiful woman they have ever seen. It is taking people time to become accustomed.'

But there was nothing reassuring in his voice. It was edged with that same tension she was feeling. Had been feeling since that explosion among the ruins and the fallout.

Yet with her hair swept up in an elaborate configuration, drop sapphire earrings hanging low, and a large sapphire framed in tiny white diamonds nestling just above her cleavage, it was true she looked a million dollars.

And no doubt was wearing that sum.

She had felt a little awkward wearing jewellery that had belonged to his grandmother, but Gianluca had assured her the pieces were so rarely worn it was almost a service to give them a showing.

As she spotted Maria Benedetti through the crowd it suddenly felt more like theft.

It was on loan. *Everything* was on loan.

Even her time with this man.

The only thing she could call her own was the dress.

Because, dammit, she had money. She'd earned it by being smart and canny and—yes—ruthless.

Why was it she couldn't be as ruthless about this man as he was clearly being with her?

'You didn't tell me your family were going to be here.'

'I didn't know.'

One glance and Ava could see the muscle ticking in his jaw. She realised Gianluca wasn't any more relaxed about this discovery than she was.

She guessed introducing her to his friends was one thing—to his family was another.

It hadn't occurred to her until she'd looked up into his beautiful face, recognised his set expression, that there had been a method in the madness of their dash from Positano to Naples, their flight from Naples to Rome.

It wasn't romantic. It was pragmatic. It was what a man did when he could feel the walls closing in around him. If the man was Gianluca Benedetti and had a jet and a *palazzo* at his command.

He'd dazzled her, wooed her, done things to her body she couldn't imagine doing with anyone else, and when this was over—whatever *this* was—he would walk away. He wouldn't be so crass as to do it by phone call, but the time would come. It wouldn't be in the near future. His desire for her was too present in their lives at this point.

This was where it was at for him. *This* was what worked for them, apparently. *This* being sex. Long-distance wasn't really going to work, then, was it?

Oh, she suspected once she was back in Sydney they would drift on a little longer together—he would fly in, she would fly out—but other women would cross his path and, really, with-

out anything stronger to bind them how long would he lie in
sheets grown cool? One day it just wouldn't work any more.

She'd accepted all this last night—told herself to toughen
up, to take it like a man. Men didn't confuse the issue. There
was sex, and there was emotional attachment, and apparently
they could exist separately. He might have given her the whole
package once, but those waters had flowed by.

But it was hard to be a tough operator in a glamorous ballgown that made her feel so intensely feminine it was all she
could do not to spin around like a little girl and send her skirts
flying just for the joy of it.

It was hard not to yearn when you found yourself swaying
to the romantic strains of Strauss as interpreted by a symphony
orchestra, dancing in the arms of the man you had longed for
all your life.

It was hard not to cry when the man you loved had had no
intention of introducing you to a single member of his family
until tonight, when he was being forced into it. He had gone
out of his way four weeks ago to make sure that couldn't possibly happen.

Oh, yes, now she knew why she'd always been so wary of
dresses. They had a way of transforming you into someone
you didn't recognise.

'My mother always gets an invitation,' Gianluca informed
her tightly, 'but this is the first time she's come.'

With the air of a man condemned Gianluca steered her
across the room. Ava became aware they were the sinecure
of every eye.

And with that the last of her confidence fell away.

She felt like a circus freak in her glamorous gown. Every
inappropriate outfit her mother had paraded in down their sub-
urban street, every time some teenager had hung out of a bus or
car window and shouted, 'Freak!,' at her mother—everything
bad about being Tiffany Lord's daughter came rushing back.

Knowing she had to keep it together, Ava stopped listening
to Gianluca's quiet instructions. As if he thought she needed

guidance on how to be with his mother. She wasn't an idiot. She knew how to behave.

Maria Benedetti looked faintly surprised as Gianluca leaned down and kissed his mother's hand. Ava noticed there was an odd stiffness between mother and son, but then the Principessa was regarding her curiously.

Gianluca introduced them and Ava heard herself offering a polite, 'How do you do?'

'Ava, how much like your brother you look. So, *you* are the young lady who has bedazzled my son?'

It wasn't what she had expected the Principessa to say and Ava immediately floundered.

'Are those the Principessa Alessandra sapphires, Gianluca?'

'Ava carries them off well,' he said tightly.

The older woman gave a insouciant shrug, eerily reminiscent of her son. 'It's nice to see them out of the vault.'

Some other conversation was going on, and Ava didn't even try to follow it. The smile pasted to her face felt paper-thin.

'You look as if you're having a wonderful time, Ava.'

'I am,' Ava lied.

'We will have lunch tomorrow, yes? I would like to know how you are enjoying Rome.'

She looked properly at Maria Benedetti and realised the woman who had so disapproved of Josh was offering her an olive branch.

'Yes, I would like that,' she fumbled, thinking of Friday. Thinking of her ticket. Thinking of the man beside her who still hadn't asked her to stay. She knew now that he wouldn't.

But she had relaxed, and she realised it probably had less to do with the Principessa and more to do with the chip on her shoulder which had been whittled down in the weeks she'd spent with Gianluca.

She wasn't standing out in this crowd. She belonged here every bit as much as Maria Benedetti.

And it wasn't just the dress. Although it helped.

Smiling a little for the first time all evening, she looked around the room, taking in the crowd—and then she saw him.

'Ava?' He lifted his hand in a half wave.

Josh appeared like a mirage in front of her, tall and thin in his tux, tugging on his bow tie.

'I can never manage these things. Alessia fiddled with it in the car and now look at it.' He wasn't quite meeting her eyes and she could see the nerves in him.

Her first instinct was to straighten it for him, but then she remembered he wasn't her little brother any more. He was a grown man. She should treat him that way.

Not even questioning why, she threw her arms around him.

He hugged her back awkwardly.

'It's okay, sis,' he muttered in her ear. 'I'll get you out of this.'

She looked at him in surprise, about to tell him there was nothing to get her out of, but instead she hugged him again. It was so good to see him. It was so good to have the courage to show him that.

The curse had been broken, she thought a little fancifully. She hadn't realised until this moment how she had carried his sentiments around with her for seven years. *Rich, disappointed and alone. I'm not going to spend my life alone and unloved*, she thought, *because no matter where life takes me my brother will always love me.*

She had a big smile on her face when a small hand touched her elbow and she recognised Alessia, five feet of crackling energy. She had hardly changed.

'Your gown is so beautiful. You look like a princess. Gianluca, she looks like a princess! Why have you been keeping her locked up? I thought we'd have to come up to Rome and break you out, Ava.'

'Gianluca has been very kind,' Ava heard herself say sincerely, and caught the look of surprise on his face.

'He *stole* you,' Alessia accused.

Well, what did she say to that?

Gianluca put a glass of champagne into her hand.

Other people joined them. Gianluca's cousin Marco and his wife, Valentina—the couple she had already met. She liked Tina. There was something down-to-earth about her that made her wish all of this were real. She would have made a good friend.

A very pregnant good friend.

'I miss champagne,' she said, indicating Ava's glass.

'It's not very good,' Ava lied.

Tina smiled and, nudging her elbow, steered her away from the group.

'I saw you being introduced to Aunt Dragon. How did it go?'

'The Principessa was most kind.'

'Really? How odd. She's usually brutal to other women. I guess it's come as a shock to her to be introduced to one of Gianluca's girlfriends.'

Ava was about to blurt out, *I'm not his girlfriend*, when Tina said cheerfully, 'In fact you're the first. You're not Sicilian, are you?'

Baffled, Ava shook her head.

Tina moved a little closer. 'A virgin?'

'Pardon?'

'No, you've got that look. That well-loved look.' The other woman gave her a little smile. 'Don't turn around, Ava, but Gianluca hasn't taken his eyes off you. I think he's worried about what I'm telling you. So I'll make it quick. He's a nightmare for women. Looks gorgeous, and he's got the title, all that money. Willing women for Gianluca are like—I don't know… ice in Siberia. Too much of a good thing, yes?'

Yes, she knew. But she felt it like another punch to her chest wall.

'I've never seen him so happy.'

'Happy?'

Gianluca stepped up to her and for a moment Ava wondered if he'd heard. He took her hand and wordlessly drew her away from the group.

'You need air,' he said, almost offhand.

Ava gave Tina a little shrug, but the other woman gave her a wink.

On the terrace he removed his jacket to cloak her shoulders. Ava shook her head, backing up.

'We need to talk.'

She was incredibly beautiful tonight.

But it wasn't like the beauty he had seen in her unguarded moments—waking up first thing in the morning, her eyes sleepy-soft, murmuring silly things to him that made him want to move mountains for her…or just kiss her.

Tonight it was a beauty that came at a cost—the kind he had grown up around. He wanted to mess up her hair, smudge her lipstick, take those heavy jewels and throw them into the Tiber.

He didn't want the Benedettis taking her over. He didn't want her to become one of those weights he carried around his neck.

'We need to talk,' she said softly.

He cleared his throat. '*Si*, this is why I have brought you out here.'

'I want to tell you something first.'

She clasped her hands together as if going to her execution.

For some reason it irritated him. But he'd been frustrated all night. He didn't want to be in a crowd with Ava. He wanted to be somewhere they could be alone, just the two of them, and then perhaps this twisting in his gut would stop.

'Have you ever seen *Three Coins in a Fountain*?' she asked unexpectedly.

He shrugged. 'Maybe. Maybe not. I know the song.'

She gave him a tentative little smile. 'I used to watch that film as a girl and I wanted that life. Some other life, so different from my own it was unrecognisable.'

With a sigh she walked away to the stone railing. Somewhere down there in the darkness the Tiber lurked.

Gianluca found himself thinking about all the carved-up

bodies of the people who had got in his ancestors' way, floating up on its banks. Where Ava saw romance he saw reality.

'You've given me that fantasy, but I think it's time to go,'
she said.

Go? She couldn't go.

'Before the spell wears off. Before you wake up one morning and I'm just Ava again.'

What in the hell…? She *was* Ava. Ava who had made him
laugh, had made him furious, had made him…*love her*.

He shoved that brutally aside. Loving her wasn't going to
work. Benedetti men didn't love their women. They bred from
them and then walked away—or as in the case of his father,
were driven away.

He'd long ago decided not to continue that nasty little tradition, but if he was going to make the mistake of his life he
might as well make it with Ava.

If she thought she was going to walk out on him he'd like
to see her try with a ring on her finger, with those heavy jewels around her neck. He'd weigh her down with so much of his
history she wouldn't be able to move.

'This life you speak of.' His voice was deep, rough-cut,
fraught with a freight load of emotion that seemed to be coming at him too fast. 'Why can't you have it?'

She looked over her shoulder at him carefully, anxiety writ-
ten in every line of her features.

As well it might be.

The ring was weighting his jacket pocket and right now it
felt like a dagger. He reached in and closed his hand over it,
made a fist of it.

'Have it, then,' he said, almost aggressively. 'Have this life.'

He reached for her and jerked her around roughly.

Ava cowered back, trying to retrieve her hand. He wasn't
letting go.

'I don't know what you're talking about. You're not making sense. Why are you angry with me?'

He took out the ring, held it up to the light.

'Does *this* make sense to you?'

For a moment she looked utterly confused, and then fell utterly still.

'This is the ring my grandfather gave to my grandmother. She only took it off on the day she died, to pass it to my eldest sister.' He took her hand; it was cold and tense in his. She tried to snatch it back but he was so much stronger. 'She chose not to use it and it's been in a vault with the rest of the family jewellery since then. I would be honoured if you—' he forced the ring over her finger, only to realise his hand was shaking, and not in a good way '—would be my wife.'

'It's too small,' she said, in an even smaller voice.

'It can be altered.' He was furious with her. Why was she cowering like that? Why was she acting as if he'd done something unforgivable when she was the one talking about fantasies and here he was fulfilling them?

She began tugging at it. 'I don't want this. Take it back.'

'Gianluca, what are you doing out here? There are people who've come halfway around the world to see you tonight. We all have to do our bit— Oh, I see I've interrupted something.'

Gianluca turned to snarl at their hostess, only to hear Ava make a choked sound of distress. With a flurry of those extravagant skirts she shoved past him and made her way back into the ballroom.

'I need help,' Ava babbled to Alessia. 'This dress won't fit in the back of a taxi and I can't go back with him. I need somewhere to stay...'

'Calm down.' Alessia stroked her arm. 'You'll come and stay with us, of course. We're in a hotel only two blocks away.'

Ava wondered why she didn't feel any better.

'What's going on, Av?' Josh was looking at her with something approaching concern.

In the past she had always fobbed him off. *She* was the protector, the one who kept the wolf from his door, but right now all she could think about was how isolated she was. She'd landed right back where she'd begun—alone in the world.

'You were right, Joshy,' she said, using her old name for him. 'I am destined to be alone.'

She couldn't stay there a moment longer. Picking up her skirts, she made her way to a set of doors. As she ran down the steps outside the *palazzo* it did cross her distressed mind that all she needed at this moment was to lose a shoe, but her Jimmy Choos were holding on as she skirted past security guards who watched as a woman in a fairy-tale dress ran out of the bright lights and into the shadowy road beyond.

Two blocks, Alessia had said.

She could run that far.

Gianluca couldn't find her.

He had made mistakes in his life. This wasn't one of them.

This was a catastrophe.

Had he really pushed a ring onto her finger?

Bullied her like that?

Whatever her reasons for being here with him, it didn't change the single, life-changing fact that he was in love with her, and he'd allowed his anger and resentment with his past to interfere in the way he had treated her.

The one person who made him want a future.

But why the hell had she said she wanted to end it?

Where the hell was she?

'Benedetti?'

Right accent. Wrong Lord sibling.

'Have you seen Ava?' he demanded.

Josh reached back and made a right-hand swing that Gianluca instinctively blocked. He shoved the younger man away.

'*Dio*, what's your problem, Lord?'

'*You're* my problem, Benedetti. You and the way you've treated my sister.'

Gianluca tensed.

'Yeah, that's right. I'm calling you on it. Some loser dumps her and you move right in. She might be smart as a whip, but she's like a deer in headlights when it comes to men.'

'*Si*, we are agreed on that.'

The younger man frowned.

'I want to marry your sister,' Gianluca said impatiently, aware that he was only wasting time. 'I'm in love with her. Does that clear things up?'

There was a sharp female intake of breath. Both Valentina and Alessia were standing behind them.

'Where is she?' asked Valentina.

'That's what I've come to tell you,' announced Alessia, clearly enjoying the drama. 'She ran out of here in a state. Possibly to our hotel.'

Gianluca was already pushing his way across the reception area, his head roaring with blood.

He was going to kill her—but only after he made sure she was all right first.

'Benedetti!' Josh Lord was breathing hard as he reached him on the steps. 'You need to hear this, man. She came to Rome expecting a proposal.'

'*Si*, she's told me,' he growled impatiently.

'No, you don't understand. She paid for the tickets, she booked the hotel, she arranged some damn fool tour of Tuscany—and she bought the ring.'

Gianluca stared at the other man as if he were speaking some language hitherto unknown.

And then he knew what he'd done.

I used to watch that film as a girl and I wanted that life. Some other life, so different from my own it was unrecognisable...

And he'd given her a shoddy proposal at a charity ball. He'd forced a ring onto her finger. He'd made a mockery of her romantic dreams after she'd confessed them to him.

If he didn't find her in the next five minutes he was going to go tear this city apart.

'She won't be at our hotel,' said Josh in a low voice. 'Not if she's hurting. When we were small, and Mum was off her meds and at her worst, Ava would take me for a walk. We'd walk to the end of the road and then she'd say, "We'll just go to the end of the next road, and the next…" as if she were looking for something. She did the same thing the night of my wedding. According to one of Alessia's friends, she didn't come back till the crack of dawn.'

With those words everything fell into place.

'*Grazie.* I know where to find her.'

I stayed there all day, hoping you'd call.

He started to run. She was on foot. He was foot. But one of them was running for his life.

The bar of The Excelsior was dark, lit here and there by lamps, but he saw her the moment he stepped inside.

Gianluca was supremely fit, so he couldn't blame the run for the heaving of his chest as his heart hammered home just how important this moment was.

The heavens had opened on the last block and his hair was plastered to his head, the shirt of his tux was damp, his jacket lost along the route. It had taken longer than it should have, for he'd had an unexpected stop, thumping on the door of Luigi Favonne. Everyone in this section of Rome knew Luigi. He could turn a diamond into living fire and for Principo Benedetti he had found, in his bed robe and bath slippers, a green emerald so true its heat licked his fingers as he held it tight in his hand.

She was sitting at the bar, her ballgown surging around her, her bare arms and shoulders above the midnight blue satin alabaster in the soft white light of the neon-lit room. The bartender was watching her as he polished glasses, and people were giving her curious looks, but no one had approached her.

She seemed to be in a world of her own.

He was within a metre of her when he said, 'Ava *mio*.'

Her head turned slowly. Her face was pale and ravaged with tears.

'I am not your Ava,' she said in a low, terrible voice. 'And I never was.'

She threw something at him. It hit him in the chest and he caught it.

The ring. The heavy, ugly, baroque ring. With all the history attached to it.

He strode up to her and stood there, resolute but unsure where to begin.

She looked up at him, her eyes furious. 'Go away. I don't want you.'

'Then why are you here, my love?'

Her chin came out. Her entire face quivered. 'I'm waiting for someone. If he's the man he should be he'll come, and if he doesn't I'm better off without him.'

He knew then how it had been for her. That long day when he'd been at the hospital with his mother and sisters, with the lawyers at the *palazzo* and with the authorities answering questions, she had been here, waiting for him to show.

Frustration shot through him. They had both made mistakes. There was nothing he could do about the past. Nothing. But he wasn't going to let it rule their lives.

In the end it came down to three words. 'I'm here now.'

She looked at him uneasily.

'I want you to forgive me, Ava. I should have moved heaven and earth to find you.'

He braced himself for whatever would come, and then, like a miracle, her chin quivered, her mouth softened and she said, 'I shouldn't have run.' Her hands spread lightly over her lap. 'You found me tonight.'

Relief shuddered through him.

She loves me, he thought. *I know she loves me.*

'And it was only one night,' she added in a low voice.

'It was our night,' he asserted. 'Our amazing perfect night.'

She looked up, something soft entering her eyes. 'It *was* perfect.'

He pocketed the old ring and extended his hand to her.

'Come with me.'

Slowly, swishing her skirts as she slid off the stool, Ava took his hand. Her soft fingers felt incredibly delicate to him and he couldn't believe he'd shoved that ring onto her finger so crudely.

He never did anything crudely. He'd been raised better. He treated women properly, with kindness and consideration. But Ava had brought other emotions to the surface—strange, rough, wild, authentic feelings. She had seen him at his worst.

She had never shied away from that.

If she would have him he would be the most fortunate man in Rome.

The Excelsior possessed a tower, built in the sixteenth century, its winding stairs well-worn from the many thousands of tourists who had climbed it since it had been restored seventy years ago.

It was roped off at this hour, but a heavy bribe enabled him access and Gianluca whisked her up the steps.

'This is crazy,' she said amidst the rustle of her gown, the heavy tread of his shoes, the click of her heels.

The view was breathtaking.

Even on this overcast night.

'Ava *mio.*' He drew her close. 'To the east of here is the Benedetti summer residence. It's old, and the drains aren't good, but every summer I would be dragged there. I hated it. I hated what it represented—hundreds of years of oppression. I vowed when I was young that I wouldn't marry, I wouldn't have children, I wouldn't continue the legacy.'

He stroked her cheek.

'Then I met you.'

Ava's black lashes were stuck starfish-fashion to her skin as she gazed up at him.

'Do you see that hill to the west? The first tribes ever to inhabit Rome lived there. I want to build a home for us there. Something that belongs only to us and our children.'

'But you don't want children.'

'I want them with you.'

Ava made a little sound.

He fell to his knees before her.

'My love, will you spend the rest of your life with me?'

She swayed slightly and before he could leap up to catch her dropped to her knees in front of him. She clutched at his shoulders. 'Oh, yes.'

He framed her precious face, kissed her temples, her eyelids, her sweet nose, her magnificent cheekbones, the full lush contours of her lips. The face he so loved.

'I love you,' he whispered. 'I loved you from the moment I first saw you in the cathedral, wearing that blue dress with the flowers in your hair. And when I saw you in the old ballroom of the *palazzo*, watching me, I thought, *It's her*.'

'Did you?' Her mouth was smiling, her lashes low.

'So I followed you.'

She shook her head. 'You made me dance with you and I couldn't dance.'

'I don't remember that. I remember I kept pulling you close and you kept trying to put space between us.'

'I didn't know you.'

'You knew enough.'

He chuckled and kissed her—really kissed her—deep and slow.

'I knew it was you that day in the street,' he muttered against her soft mouth. 'I just didn't know I knew.'

'I came to Rome to find you,' she confessed. 'Although I didn't know it at the time.'

It was some minutes before he remembered what was burning a hole in his shirt pocket.

He reached in and extracted the stone, gently laid it in her palm.

Green fire.

'I will have this made into a ring for you, Ava *mio*. It will be yours. *Ours*.'

She looked into his eyes, her heart shining in them.

When they emerged into the street below the rain had stopped, but the roads were wet and there was a pungent smell in the air. He didn't have a jacket to give her, and it wasn't warm, but he was taking her somewhere that didn't matter.

'Where are we going, Benedetti?'

'I thought we'd walk for a while, Ava *mio*, find a little church and get married.'

'Can we do that?' Her voice floated up among the pigeons roosting in the window grooves above them.

'Well, there are banns to be read, and the matter of your citizenship, and I suspect the priest will be in his bed at this hour...' Gianluca drew her in close against him. 'Then again, *innamorata*, this is Rome.'

'Yes,' sighed Ava, resting her head over his heart. 'Anything's possible.'

* * * * *

Mills & Boon® Hardback
November 2013

ROMANCE

Million Dollar Christmas Proposal	Lucy Monroe
A Dangerous Solace	Lucy Ellis
The Consequences of That Night	Jennie Lucas
Secrets of a Powerful Man	Chantelle Shaw
Never Gamble with a Caffarelli	Melanie Milburne
Visconti's Forgotten Heir	Elizabeth Power
A Touch of Temptation	Tara Pammi
A Scandal in the Headlines	Caitlin Crews
What the Bride Didn't Know	Kelly Hunter
Mistletoe Not Required	Anne Oliver
Proposal at the Lazy S Ranch	Patricia Thayer
A Little Bit of Holiday Magic	Melissa McClone
A Cadence Creek Christmas	Donna Alward
Marry Me under the Mistletoe	Rebecca Winters
His Until Midnight	Nikki Logan
The One She Was Warned About	Shoma Narayanan
Her Firefighter Under the Mistletoe	Scarlet Wilson
Christmas Eve Delivery	Connie Cox

MEDICAL

Gold Coast Angels: Bundle of Trouble	Fiona Lowe
Gold Coast Angels: How to Resist Temptation	Amy Andrews
Snowbound with Dr Delectable	Susan Carlisle
Her Real Family Christmas	Kate Hardy